SHIFTERS FOR THE HOLIDAY

SEDONA VENEZ

WANT FREE SEDONA VENEZ BOOKS?

Sign up for Sedona Venez's Newsletter and receive FREE BOOKS. In addition to the free stories, you will also get special pricing, exclusive previews and news of new releases.

GET A FREE SEDONA VENEZ BOOK!

Join Sedona's mailing list to be the first to know of new releases, free books, special prices and other author giveaways.

https://sedonavenez.com/free-book

Get Warm and Fuzzy. New Holiday Romance Story That'll Give You All The Feels...

Someone wants me dead... This is not going to be a very Merry Christmas.

If arsonists setting fire to my barn right before Christmas isn't bad enough, a sniper shooting through my bedroom window is like getting a lump of coal for Christmas.

But I don't want protection. My father thinks otherwise and hires two rugged former military wolf-shifters—Axel and Tucker—to protect me at all costs.

But I'm not your ordinary damsel in distress. I'm a curvy, independent woman, used to running things my way. But when I'm trapped inside my cabin with my gorgeous bodyguards during a blizzard, sensual boundaries are crossed, leaving me attracted to not one, but both of my wolf-shifter protectors.

Now, not only is my life on the line, but so is my heart...

This passionate stand-alone Christmas story is full of festive magic, romance, suspense, and laughs. HEA and no cliffhanger!

❧   I   ❧

I sat down on the old leather couch, dropping my boot-clad feet onto the coffee table. Normally, I would have yelled at anyone who did that, but right now, all I could think of was easing my aching soles.

It was the middle of December. The first sheep were dropping their lambs. It seemed earlier than last year, but it always seemed too early, too cold, for those little bundles of black and white to be born. I wanted them to arrive in sunshine and warmth, but they always seemed to be born in the middle of the coldest night, during the worst weather.

Wintering lambs were not tough. Having them spend their most delicate days in a warm, sheltered barn with their mothers was better for them than wandering muddy spring pastures, especially since the forest surrounded my land, and early spring was the hungriest season for predators. But the lambing itself was hard on everyone, especially me.

I leaned my head on the back of the couch and looked up at the galaxy of Christmas lights hanging from the ceiling beams, splashing multicolored glow down on the dim room. Elizabeth had gone a little hog-wild with the decorations again. She loved Christmas and wanted to teach me to love it too, but my family's endless awkward holidays trained me out of that. I got depressed instead. Being super busy with the lambing helped with keeping my mind off the dark and lonely days when I was expected to fit in by pretending to be merry and bright.

Outside, it was spitting something between rain and snow. There was a bite to the wind that told me it was probably going to turn colder. If it did, we'd have an ice-covered world by morning, which would mean I would slip all over the place when I let the horses out for their normal wander around the pasture.

I'd dressed down for working in the barns, in sun-faded jeans that clung to my curves and a pale-blue flannel top that popped against my dark skin. I tied my loose black curls back behind a handkerchief to keep them from tangling in the sharp, icy wind. When I reached up to my cheek, it was to brush a curl of bedding shavings off it. The smell of sheep and birthing blood still clung to the insides of my nostrils.

Nine days until Christmas, and instead of relaxing to prepare for the festive holidays, I was delivering unexpectedly early lambs. The delivery of the sheep involved a lot more risk, especially with the weather so crappy that a veterinarian might not get here in time in an emergency.

I really shouldn't worry so much. The sheep knew what they were doing, aside from the few new moms I checked on each hour. The others that were in the barn just looked at me placidly, waiting for me to go away so they could get on with what they knew how to do. They were calmer about the yearly mess than I was.

Maybe that was because lambing wasn't the only yearly mess I was dealing with right now. If the lambing and the storm had worn me out physically, the "holiday season" was doing so emotionally. I didn't technically celebrate, beyond sending gifts and having a nice dinner with my staff and some friends, but some people in my life just wouldn't leave it alone.

Today had been a day for arguments, with Dad and Marcie, his latest trophy wife, tag-teaming me with tense phone calls over my decision to once again skip their glittering Christmas celebration in DC. It shouldn't have been a surprise to Dad, even if Marcie—a vapid ex-starlet only four years older than me—was too new to our dysfunctional family situation to figure out why.

I hadn't flown down to DC in five years. Dad knew the reasons. He knew to expect that I would do anything to avoid the scumbags he cozied up to at those damn holiday parties. It was never just about family, or Christmas, for him. It was about impressing his donors and his buddies on Capitol Hill. And that included showing off his daughter to them. The last time I had gone to his party, I'd had way too many greedy-eyed forty-, fifty-, and sixty-year-old DC bastards asking me if I was married or single and available. While Dad stood back and smiled like a king trying to turn his troublesome daughter into a strategic asset in one of his alliances.

Ugh. No. Never again.

No matter how much he lectured and tried to bark orders. No matter how much his latest too-young piece of ass tried to sound like a shocked and disappointed mother. But Dad was stubborn and arrogant, and so we had the same damn argument every single year. This year, today had been the day. The timing was just shittier than usual.

I closed my eyes, thinking about what I could eat that didn't require any energy to make. Or didn't require me to get up off the couch. The fire Elizabeth had lit in the enormous fireplace was throwing off a lot of heat, and it made me sleepy. When I thought about it, food could wait. Sleep was more of a priority. I ached all over, and moving again just didn't seem like an option.

Without opening my eyes, I pulled my massive, soft velvet throw blanket off the back of the couch, wrapped it around me and curled into the corner of my big, comfy sofa. I didn't even care that I was still in my boots.

The sound of the back door slamming against the kitchen wall, and someone yelling my name, made me bolt upright. I was dizzy from being yanked out of slumber and did not understand what time it was. Glancing around, I saw it was still dark out. *What's going on?*

I was totally disoriented, but I knew that male voice—Henry, my strong right hand at Stone's Throw Ranch. It was his tone that was unfamiliar—loud and harsh. He almost sounded panicked.

Oh God, now what?

I threw the blanket off myself and ran toward the kitchen. One foot had fallen asleep from lying down on the sofa in my boots, and I stumbled painfully for a few steps until the feeling came back to my feet.

Henry was standing in the kitchen, his leathery, sun-darkened face streaked with soot and red in patches. The look in his dark eyes told me he had nothing but bad news for me.

My heart skipped a beat as I realized that the entire world smelled of woodsmoke. There was a fire. *A fire on my land!*

He confirmed it a second later, his voice harsh with urgency. "Miss Glory, it's the barn."

"Oh my God. The sheep?" If it was the sheep, the babies could never get out, and their mothers would never leave them. They would all burn together.

"No. It's the horse barn."

That didn't help my fears. It just shifted them. I grabbed my sheepskin jacket from the pegs by the door, shrugging into it as I followed Henry into the dark. My limbs still ached from exhaustion, but I forced myself through the door, adrenaline and determination fueling my every move.

The rain had turned to slushy snow, and I cursed under my breath. Rain might have helped keep the fire down, but snow was pretty much useless. The rising heat would send it swirling away from the barn like feathers in a breeze.

I saw a sickly yellow glow dancing against the trees. Then we rounded the corner of the house, and the world was suddenly lit with dark orange and yellow flames. Smoke billowed across the pasture, mixing with the blowing slush.

"Oh God," I wheezed, shock and horror pushing all the air from my lungs.

"I called 9-1-1 from the sheep barn when I saw the flames!" Henry shouted over his shoulder as we ran toward the barn. "They'll be here as soon as they can."

I was only half listening. My heart was pounding in my ears as I thought of my small herd of horses panicking in their stalls as the place burned around them.

The enormous structure was almost engulfed as flames danced against the black sky. My heart stopped, then started up again in a jittery beat, the extra rush of adrenaline turning my limbs to jelly. I wanted to be sick in the snow, but that wouldn't help anyone.

I gulped smoky air to calm myself but only ended up coughing. "Oh God. The horses..."

A huge, callused hand settled on my shoulder. "I got them out, Alina. It's okay. They all ran off toward the far pasture."

I turned to Henry. He'd called me by my first name. I saw, besides the soot and wind-chapping, there were red burns on his face and on his big, rough hands. *Oh no. He ran into that inferno to free them.* Because, of course, he had. That was just how he was.

"Henry..." I put my hand on his arm. There was nothing else I could say. He'd saved my horses, the loves of my life. It should have been me doing that. But I had worn myself out during my shift with the sheep.

"You're blaming yourself," he chided gently. He could tell. Henry never missed much. "Don't."

"Hard not to," I sighed, trying to peer past the burning barn into the darkness of the field. The horses must have run that way. I only hoped that none of them had injured themselves in their panic. I would have to examine them when this craziness was over.

Think about that. Think past this disaster, past the horror, past wondering how this happened, to what you need to do once it's over. You can't control that there's a fire. You can only control your response.

Minutes passed like hours as we waited for the first responders to show, then Henry raised his head, peering off into the distance.

"There are the fire trucks." He pointed toward the horizon, lights flashing where the spur road came off from the highway. As the crow flew, we were dead center between New Fane and Jenner's Falls, but the roads cut back and forth across the mountain between here and there. Still, the fire department had made good time, even with the foul weather. *Thank God.*

The first big truck, with New Fane in gold letters on the side, drove up the driveway and across the yard, followed by a water truck. The team jumped out, and in seconds, men were pulling hoses off the trucks, making connections, turning them on, water spraying over the flames. A second truck from Jenner's Falls arrived a few minutes later, with its own water tanker.

Henry and I stood in the house's lee, watching, helpless to do anything, as the fire fought back against the men working to put it out. Everything had taken on a surreal feeling, like watching a movie of someone else's barn burning down. And thanks to the shock, it felt like I was watching it all in slow motion.

How could this have happened?

There was a ton of flammable stuff in any barn—hay, straw, wood chips, grain. But the electrical system was only a few years old. We had no space heaters going, and we didn't use any kind of fire source. Nor did Henry or I smoke. He had a cigar now and again, but never anywhere near the barn.

There was another possibility, one that horrified me even more to contemplate. I pushed it out of my head. I would not let myself jump to conclusions like arson. Until I had facts, there was no point scaring myself.

"Looks like they're getting it under control." Henry pointed, and I tried to see what he saw, how he could tell among the chaos playing out in front of us what was happening. But all I saw were flames that didn't seem anywhere near ready to quit. They towered over the trucks as they devoured my barn. The streams of water could have been from squirt guns for all the good they seemed to do. The firefighters had to shout to one another above their roar, which was making my ears hurt.

"You think so?" I hugged myself, shivering, not from cold, but from adrenaline and fear and whatever else was running through me. My stomach, already gnawing from emptiness, now felt full of acid.

"Yeah. I do." In an uncharacteristic gesture, he put his arm around me, hugging me roughly against him.

It startled me into silence. In the five years Henry Marvin Foster had been my ranch foreperson, he'd shown no familiarity with me, aside from shaking my hand on the day I'd hired him. He still called me Miss Glory, even though I'd asked him to call me Alina more times than I could remember. He was a man apart, not distant so much as self-contained. He knew his job and he did it, and that was that.

But this wasn't a regular day at the ranch. Something beyond terrible had happened. And he knew it, so the regular rules were set aside.

I was pathetically grateful for it. A side-hug from him felt like a hug from a dad should have. Not that I knew much about that, but I was grateful as hell for his warm strength right now.

Heavy footsteps sloshed toward us across the field, only becoming audible as they got close. "Alina Glory?"

I turned toward the voice, looking up at the mountain of a man in a bulky jacket with a New Fane police patch on the pocket. Next to him was another New Fane officer, almost as tall, almost as broad. Both were brown-haired, dark-eyed, and slightly shaggy-looking, despite their uniforms, with craggy good looks. Together, they looked like a section of Saddle Peak had broken off, split in half, and landed in my yard. Despite my shock, I tried not to stare.

"Yes." Henry's arm dropped from me, and momentarily, I wished it hadn't. But I squared my shoulders and stepped forward. "I'm Alina Glory."

The one speaking offered me a tight smile that didn't touch his small black eyes. "I'm Officer Taylor, and this is Officer Hastings. We're with the New Fane Police Department." They positively loomed over me, but not menacingly—more like a wall between me and the fire. I wasn't sure, but it seemed like that might be deliberate. It put me just a little more at ease.

I reached out, shaking the hands offered. Callused hands like Henry's, but twice again as big, with a strength in them I would have found alarming in different circumstances. They weren't rough, but I could smell a musk coming off them, powerful enough that it rose above the woodsmoke. It smelled a little familiar. My eyes narrowed slightly, but I didn't comment on it.

"Do you know how the fire started?" Taylor asked. "Are there any portable heaters running? Cigarettes? Anything?"

I shook my head. "No. There are space heaters running in the sheep barn." I pointed over my shoulder to the small building on the other side of the yard. I gave a brief prayer of thanks that the buildings were not connected. "But the horses didn't need any extra." The barn had been snug...while it had stood. Now, a few walls were still up, but I could already tell it was completely gutted inside. I wondered if even the frame would stand by the end.

"The sheep barn's not involved." Henry caught himself investigating the burns on his face with his fingers and dropped his hands. "I was in there dealing with lambing. That's why I was up to notice the fire."

Yeah, we were lucky. If he had gone home to his wife and kids as usual, my horses would be dead now.

"I guess lambing started early this year." Officer Hastings shook his head. "It always manages to lamb during the worst weather."

That got him a small smile, though I barely had the strength for it. "Yes. Always." I was not surprised to find out he was familiar with the ranches around here. Most of our cops were local. The communities around here were pretty insular.

"Once this is under control, we're going to talk to the fire marshal, have him take a quick look around. I'd also like to walk the grounds before I go." Hastings opened a small notebook. "Sorry to ask, but were there any horses inside?"

"No. Henry, my ranch foreperson, got them out safely."

Taylor looked up, a look of startled admiration on his face. "Takes some kind of man to do that. You all right?"

"Only thing I could do." Henry looked humble and proud at the same time. "Got a little singed, but my conscience would have burned me harder than the fire."

"Best to let the paramedic check you out, just in case. Can I get your full name?" Taylor wrote Henry's answer, and I had no choice but to smile at Henry's hesitation over his middle name. *Marvin.* Family name, he'd said. *Thorn in his side*, I thought.

Taylor turned back to me. His partner seemed content to let him do most of the talking, but I could see his bright eyes sweeping around, taking in us, the burning building, and everything else he could in the dark. "Did you notice anyone, see anyone around? I know it's dark, and you've been focused on the sheep..."

I shook my head. "No, nothing." What did he think might have happened?

Henry shrugged. "The dogs were barking down in the kennels, but they bark all the time. We get coyotes, foxes, bears... You know how it goes. Anyway, I came out of the sheep barn over there to take a breather, and I saw the fire. I called 9-1-1 on my cell, and then opened the door, let the horses out, and ran to get Miss Glory."

"You were in the house?" Taylor turned to me.

I watched Officer Hastings walk toward the barn, giving it a wide berth, circling off into the darkness. He wasn't using a flashlight. Like the smell, it pricked at my mind, putting me on alert.

His outline quickly blended with the shadows, only growing visible again when the firelight licked over it. The light was darker orange now, the flames lower, grudgingly giving up the fight.

"Ma'am?" Taylor prodded.

"Yes. I'd checked the sheep, then came in and fell asleep. Henry woke me up," I answered distractedly. *Where was the guy going? And why hadn't he said anything to his partner about it?*

Taylor wrote down my answers, then closed his notebook. "Okay. For now, stay out of the barn until the fire marshal looks at it. It's not safe, and we need to make sure there was no foul play. Where can we reach you?"

I gave him the ranch number and my cell. "I'm not going anywhere anytime soon." I just hoped I could find the horses a nearby place to board until we could rebuild. The spaces I had for them to winter here were just too damn small, especially for my giant stallion.

Officer Taylor nodded, tucking the notebook into his jacket pocket. Then he gave me that look most local people did, after they thought about my last name, that we were in Montana, and the lightbulb went on.

"Are you related to Senator Glory?"

Crap. "He's my father. We're not exactly close." I hoped the tone of my voice would keep him from asking any more questions about my family. Most folks did, and it set my teeth on edge.

"I'll make a note of that. Probably no connection, but you never know."

The other officer was back. There was something different about his posture, the look on his face. The hair on the back of my neck started prickling. Red flag. But he said nothing. He just nodded politely to me, and the two turned around and walked back to their patrol car.

"Something's up," I muttered. "They found something." I wanted to know what that something was. *Had someone burned down my barn after all? Who? And why? And why had they walked away without even talking about it?*

"Yeah. I think the same. But they said we're supposed to stay away from the barn. We should just..."

"When have you ever done what you're supposed to do when your gut tells you differently? You weren't supposed to run into a burning barn either, but my horses are alive because you did. Get a flashlight."

I didn't like some cop walking my land, finding something, and then not letting me in on what that something was. It said he didn't trust me. It made me wonder if they considered me a suspect. And I wasn't about to wait placidly and ignorantly while something went on under my nose on my own property.

Maybe I had a problem with authority. But I had gotten nowhere by going along with what people in charge told me. If I had, I would have ended up some gross old politician's miserable trophy wife.

Henry snorted. "You sure? We disturb something, those guys will notice. I'm sure of it." But he didn't sound too worried. In fact, he was smiling faintly.

"Then we won't disturb anything. Look, those guys aren't talking, and if someone did something to my property, I want to know about it." And anyway, the cop hadn't gone near the barn. He had gone around it, well away from the fire crews.

Henry nodded and disappeared into the house, reappearing a few minutes later with a high-powered flashlight. The patrol car had backed out of the driveway, and the only people here were inside the shell of the barn, hosing down the embers until the last of them cooled.

"We just walk where he did, in his tracks, and we'll be okay." I took the light, shining it over the dirty snow, following a set of boot prints even bigger than Henry's. Fat flakes were falling now, and they would soon cover up our tracks, removing any evidence that we had walked out this way. But soon enough, the cop's trail would be gone too, and we would lose it entirely if we didn't move fast.

The flames were out now, the timbers of the barn rising like the blackened ribs of some giant beast. Along the edges of the ashes, flashlights flickered in and out of the burned timber as the firefighters worked the site. We let them work, not going near. But we didn't really have to in order to follow the trail.

The officer's tracks cut a wide circle around the barn. I walked ahead, searching for the next print with my flashlight, Henry striding along behind me. The tracks meandered a little where Hastings had looked at whatever had caught his attention. We followed them, and then they stopped. Suddenly, abruptly, they were no more.

Had I lost them? The snow was thickening; it was possible. I shone the light around worriedly. Then suddenly, I found something. It just wasn't at all what I had expected.

"What the hell? Look at this," I said.

Henry stepped up beside me, looking at where I pointed the light. There were big boot tracks and then a flurry of displaced snow. Then, several feet away, were the unmistakable tracks of a bear. An enormous one.

"Huh... That must have been what got the dogs all riled up. Haven't seen a bear down here in a long time." Not since the last drought, in fact, when hunger and thirst had brought them down the mountain to forage. Henry had seen one wandering across our pasture one night, sniffing after the scent of our sheep. He had brought me the warning and then sat at the barn window with his shotgun for the rest of the night.

I played the light ahead of us. The bear tracks went behind the barn, then disappeared into the dark, heading for the woods. The snow covered them completely before we could follow them farther.

Ah crap, my horses are out there with no proper shelter, and now we have a damn bear sniffing around.

Henry must have read my mind. "We should go back. We might disturb evidence. And that bear might still nose around, looking for dinner."

I looked up at him. He was worried about something, but I

wasn't sure it was something to do with the fire or the bear. At any rate, he was right. There wasn't anything here we could find that the officer hadn't already seen. "Okay. Can you get the horses into shelter? Put them in the empty sheep stalls. Nowhere else will be big enough. I don't want them in the open in this mess, especially with a bear around." *Or a damn arsonist.*

"Got it. Try to eat if you can and get some rest. You're practically staggering."

He was right. I was even more exhausted now than I had been when I had fallen asleep with my boots on. I guessed it was the adrenaline...though my discovery just now had helped little.

We walked back through the snow, each wrapped up in our own thoughts. He muttered something that sounded like goodnight and turned toward the sheep barn. He'd make another check on my girls and then do what he could for the horses. I knew he would get the job done to the best of his ability. Henry was a rock, even when the weather, lambing, wildlife, accidents, and possibly one of my neighbors were unreliable and unpredictable.

I'd come out at dawn and see how they were. I also knew he'd be spending the rest of the night sitting in the sheep barn, or somewhere close by, with his double-barrel shotgun across his lap, just in case the bear or the arsonist, if there was one, came back for another visit.

I hung up my jacket and wandered around the kitchen for a minute, too keyed up to think straight about fixing food. My horse barn had burned to the ground, along with a loft full of hay and an assortment of other things I couldn't even remember right now.

The horses were okay. They were out in the weather, but they knew enough to take care of themselves until Henry could get them under cover for the night. Hopefully, this mess would blow over, and we could let them out once the sunlight softened up any ice. I didn't want to deal with injured horses on top of everything else.

I thought about Henry in the dark, waiting for the bear to come back or to go after the horses. More than anything, I wanted to tell him it was the least of our problems right now. But I couldn't.

Because that bear really wasn't a bear. He was potentially a lot more dangerous. Or, more accurately, that bear was Officer Hastings, who was a bear-shifter.

2

The next morning, I woke up on the couch again, in the same clothes from last night. At least I had taken off my boots this time. I blinked up at my living room ceiling, wondering why I was so stiff and had such a headache. Then last night came back to me, and I sighed, gingerly sitting up.

Time to face the day, however little I was looking forward to it.

Outside, the world was all gray and white, the light casting a silvery haze over everything. The ice storm I had predicted had turned into snow instead, with only the area around the barn too slippery for the horses. They didn't seem to want to go near it anyway; outside the kitchen window, I could see the herd circled together against the chill at the far end of the pasture. Henry had apparently been unsuccessful in rounding them up, but they looked all right, and I tried not to worry.

Everything was weirdly calm after last night's chaos. If I didn't look at the burned skeleton of my horse barn, I could almost forget about the fire. Except, of course, for the acrid smell of smoke still lingering around the property. It was thick and made my nose sting, and there was no getting away from it, even indoors. I looked away from the barn, down the drive, noticing the tracks from the fire trucks last night were not much more than soft ruts in the newly fallen snow.

It was going to be a day of phone calls to insurance companies and of trying to pick through the ruins, looking for anything to salvage. Then it occurred to me I'd have to deal with cleaning up this mess too. And that was too much to think about right now.

At least I had decent insurance. It might not cover site cleanup, but beyond my deductible, it would probably cover everything else. I hoped.

Henry was sitting on a bench by the door to the sheep barn, shotgun across his knees, blinking his reddened eyes slowly as he struggled not to nod off. I held out the mug of coffee I'd brought, and he set down the rifle, leaning it against the building.

"Did anything happen out there worth mentioning last night?" I wasn't sure if I was asking about the sheep...or something else.

Henry shook his head, almost inhaling the scalding hot coffee. When he came up for air, he looked up at me. "Nope. No bears, no trespassers, and the dogs stayed quiet. Fiona dropped a ewe and a buck, though."

Even with my headache, I had to smile. Fiona was my latest acquisition, a petite Jacob sheep, the smallest of the herd. I had been hesitant to breed her, but she was a purebred, and I wanted to increase the herd. Now, she had given me twins. It was a stroke of luck in the middle of a really shitty morning.

He smiled lopsidedly over the rim of his mug. "For such a tiny thing, she had no trouble at all."

I patted Henry on the shoulder. "You sat with her, didn't you?" There were dark circles under his eyes, but I knew Henry well enough to know he'd have stayed awake no matter what. Between the fire, the lambing, and the horses being loose during the ongoing threat of what he thought was a bear, he wouldn't have slacked off. He never did.

"She didn't need me, but I hung around just in case." He got up, set the mug on the empty bench, and stretched what must have been monumentally stiff joints. "Come on, let's go look. Did you get any sleep?"

I shook my head. "I dozed off on the couch for maybe an hour. That was kind of it. Too much adrenaline."

"Yeah, I get that. I didn't even feel sleepy until after dawn broke. I must knock off for a while this afternoon once we get the horses dealt with."

I forced a smile. "Of course. You've more than earned it. Thank you for everything."

The lambs were up and moving, which lifted my heart. Fiona was attentive, both to them and to her feed. All good signs. We stood for a minute, shoulder to shoulder, a little like grandparents at the nursery window of a hospital.

A few minutes into my looking the sheep over, I caught Henry stifling a yawn. "Go get some sleep, Henry. I'll go find the horses and get them fed."

His brow furrowed. "You'll need help. Storm won't come without some persuasion."

"Storm is an old softy, you know that." I was half joking, though. He was probably right.

Storm was a big black ranch horse, mean as hell when he had it in his head, but with the heart of a warrior and the stamina to climb mountains. He was the major reason that I rarely feared for my small herd; he could kill coyotes with one blow of his hoof, and he had. He'd come in if he had a mind, or if not, he'd hunker down out there. But I wanted him in, not so much for his safety, but for my peace of mind.

"Maybe he'll follow Mary and Jane." The girls would come to feed rattled in a bucket. They behaved like sensible horses.

"He'll do as he pleases." Henry muttered something else, but it faded away as we turned toward the horse barn. Or, more accurately, to the ruined, charred mass that had been the horse barn. Any joy I'd felt seeing the lambs blew away on the frosty morning wind. *Dammit. It's a total loss, and I still don't know why it happened.*

"I'll get the feed." I pivoted away, headed for the metal feed shed. I grabbed a bucket, dumped some grain in, and closed the door. My eyes were stinging, and I took a few deep breaths before coming back out, not wanting Henry to see me teary-eyed.

Henry had tromped over to the back of the barn, and I followed his big boot tracks. I could hear horse sounds, and as I came around the corner of the barn, Mary and Jane were dancing nervously, tossing their heads, but coming to Henry's soft whistle. Storm was nowhere to be seen. *Of course. Big, adorable pain in my ass.*

I rattled the pail, and both girls' ears perked up. They came closer, giving the barn a wide berth. I could see their nostrils flare whenever the wind shifted and blew the barn's acrid smell toward us. Steeling myself, I grabbed Mary's halter, and Henry caught Jane, and we led them to the sheep barn. There were a few empty stalls that would work for the time being. Too small for them to winter in, but they would do for now.

"Do you see him anywhere?" I looked back over my shoulder. The wind kept picking up and blowing veils of snow across the pasture, hiding parts of it from sight.

He shook his head, squinting into the distance. "He's out there, though. I heard him whinny."

I nodded. "You take the girls and finish clearing him a stall. I'll go get him."

Henry disappeared into the sheep barn, and I took the pail and went back to the pasture. I hiked halfway across the field before I finally peered ahead and sighed with relief. In the distance, I could see Storm's black form against the snow. He tossed his head when I shook the pail, but he came no closer.

"So, we're going to play hard to get? Fine." I trudged out across the field, shaking the bucket. I'd gotten three-quarters of the way across the field when he turned his head, gave me a look, and then trotted over, nuzzling the bucket.

"You're just a big tease, you know that?" I grabbed his halter, and he let me lead him back to the sheep barn. He balked at going in, probably spooked by the faint blood smells of the lambing, but I rattled the little bit of feed in the pail, and he changed his mind. The stalls would need proper setting up before we were done, but at least the horses were now out of the cold and able to drink and fill their bellies.

I tucked him away in the last stall, then made a final check of my sheep. They all looked healthy, although a little confused over their new neighbors.

Storm snorted and turned around uncomfortably in his too-small stall. "Sorry, buddy, but the temperature's dropping again. I'll let you out once it's warmer." *Yeah, I really need to find a place to board them sooner rather than later.* Yet more phone calls to make. *Ugh.*

Henry was in the yard, watching a car coming up the drive. Elizabeth Torres, my housekeeper, ranch cook—and substitute mother figure—pulled up and parked. She got out slowly, eyes as dark as mine showing whites all around from horror as she looked between me and the barn.

Oh shit. I forgot to let her know. I wished then I'd remembered to call her, so she wouldn't learn about the fire by seeing the ruined barn. *Oh great. And of course, I remember just now.*

"Alina? What happened?" Her eyes locked on the barn as she stumbled through the ruts in the drive, walking more or less in my direction. I met her and put my arm around her shoulder.

"It was a fire, Elizabeth. Late last night. Henry got the horses out." I squeezed her and realized she was shaking. She was short and sturdy, and ordinarily, there didn't seem to be anything that fazed her. Except, apparently, for the sight of the burned barn.

I could hardly blame her for that. Every time I looked at it, I started worrying again that I would break down in front of them.

"It's okay. There's insurance on the barn and the stuff. And the horses are okay. And we have new lambs." I smiled, hoping that would cheer her up a little.

She turned to me. "You have to be exhausted, you and Henry. Knowing you, you were up all night." She pulled away, heading for the house, determination and motherly instincts kicking in. "You get cleaned up, and I'll start breakfast."

Henry was already walking through the slushy snow to the house, and I started after them. Elizabeth's breakfasts were legendary, and even though I was exhausted and needed to make phone calls, all that could wait. We trooped into the kitchen, shedding boots and jackets. Only then did I notice that the stink from the fire hadn't inundated the inside of my house. Instead, it was clinging to my clothes.

"I'm going to grab a quick shower and change clothes." I bounded up the stairs, heading for my room. It felt weirdly chilly in the upstairs hallway, but I didn't realize why until I walked into my bedroom.

I opened the door. Icy wind whistled through a broken window, a few flakes of snow blowing across my bed. *Oh...crap.*

For a moment, I just stood there, not sure what to do. *How the hell could I have a broken window?* In my sleep-deprived state, I tried to make a connection between the fire and this, but the barn was on the other side of the house. I couldn't remember any kerosene tanks or anything else blowing up that could have thrown debris through my window anyway. I stood in the doorway, too tired to think, much less move. *How the hell did this happen?*

Then I saw the hole in the wall above my bed. My eyes widened. *Oh God.*

I'd been hunting enough times to recognize a bullet hole. A heavy caliber one, at that.

I backed into the hallway, staring at the wall. From a safe distance, I reached out, pulling the door closed. It latched with a soft click, and the sound galvanized me into action.

I took the stairs at a dead run, came around the corner into the kitchen, and promptly bounced off a confused-looking Henry. He grunted as my shoulder contacted his sternum, but he caught me before I went down on my ass.

"Alina! What on earth?" Elizabeth turned from the stove, a spatula in one hand.

"Miss? What's wrong?" Henry righted me, and I stumbled past him, grabbing the back of the nearest kitchen chair for support. My legs had turned rubbery, and the world had gone a little fuzzy around the edges.

"Someone shot through my bedroom window. Right at my bed. If I had been in it...it would have..." *It would have hit me. In the goddamn head.*

Once I said the words, it was more real. *Very real.* I pulled the chair out from the table and dropped into it.

"Shot? Now? I heard nothing. Are you hurt?" Elizabeth dropped the spatula, crossing the kitchen and sitting down beside me. Behind her, a thin curl of smoke rose from whatever was burning in the skillet. Henry reached over and turned off the burner, edging the pan off the heat.

"No. It must have been last night. I slept down here, on the couch. I was too tired to go upstairs." And if I hadn't... If I had gotten up to go to bed like I had intended—like I did every night—that bullet might well have ended up in my skull. *Oh God.*

Henry had retrieved the phone from the hall, and I could hear him talking, his voice low. When he put the phone down, his face was the gravest I'd seen in a long time.

"Called the cops. They're sending someone out from New Fane. They'll be here shortly. Said not to touch anything."

I nodded. The numb feeling was leaving my limbs as I thought about when this could have happened. As for whoever had done it, their identity was way beyond anything I could comprehend. I just didn't have enemies like that—at least, not ones who used guns.

Well, that tears it. Someone tried to kill me last night. And the fire happening at the same time couldn't be a coincidence.

The scenario played over again in my head. Someone with a rifle, waiting out there in the dark, firing through my window after watching me go into the house to get some rest, and then setting the fire. Why the second, I didn't know.

"Hell of a Christmas present," Henry muttered disgustedly. "I'm so sorry."

I let out a hysterical little laugh. I could already predict what Dad was going to say about this. "The twin lambs were a Christmas present. This is some bastard taking a giant crap all over our lives." And I still didn't know why.

A burned barn.

A bullet through my window.

Who would do this? Why?

I just didn't have any answers. I could only hope that the cops found one. But I would not hold my breath.

Elizabeth got up and poured us coffee, and we sat drinking it in silence until we heard the siren outside in the yard.

❧ 3 ☙

My doorway filled with bear-shifter cops, the same pair again instead of a new one.

Once I had greeted them and fortified them with some of Elizabeth's rocket-fuel coffee, we got right down to business. Officer Hastings sat at the kitchen table, writing what Henry had to tell him, which wasn't much, just a continuation of last night's events. I went upstairs with Officer Taylor, who brought his mug with him.

He stood in the doorway to my room, taking in every inch of the space with sharp eyes. I stood back, bracing myself for the questions. I just hoped the attempt on my life would keep him from being so tight-lipped about answering my own.

"You said you slept on the couch?" He finally turned back to me. I nodded.

"After the sheep, and then the fire, I was so tired that I just crashed downstairs on the sofa. I couldn't even get up the stairs. Now I feel like that was lucky." The first time, my exhaustion had saved my life. The second, it had spared me a nasty shock when I could have handled it the least.

And depending on whether the would-be sniper had still been around, possibly another bullet. The thought made me shudder. Not to mention, made me want to sleep down in my basement from now on.

He nodded once. "When was the last time you were up here?" He had his little notebook out, waiting for my answer.

He didn't blink enough. I knew why. It was one habit that helped me pick out shifters. Their males, especially the ones in charge, hated breaking eye contact too much. Probably a dominance thing.

"Yesterday morning, probably an hour past dawn. I got dressed and then went downstairs. This was the first time I'd been back up here since then." I shivered. The sight of that bullet hole between the bars of my brass headboard still scared the hell out of me. *Who did this? And why?* My imagination tried to fill in the blanks, but nothing I could come up with made any sense.

He nodded. "I have to ask, do you have any enemies, Miss Glory?"

I shook my head. "No one I know of. At least, not among the neighbors. We all get along pretty well. There's a broken fence once in a while, a few stray cattle that tromp through the corn, or a horse that jumps the pasture fence. Usually my stallion." I tried to force a wry smile, but it just wouldn't come. "But it's nothing anyone would want to take a shot at me for." Unless one of them was secretly very crazy. Or had a guest over for Christmas, some distant cousin or something, who was.

He nodded, made a note, and then fixed me with those steely black eyes. "You've got a bit of a reputation as a hothead. At least, that's the rumor in New Fane."

For a moment, I was speechless, and then I laughed. There was a hysterical note to it I couldn't control any more than the laughter. *A hothead? That was their impression? Jesus.* "I guess that's what that whiny bully and his buddies call someone who fights back at all."

Taylor cocked an eyebrow at me but stayed quiet.

"I got in a minor argument with Shamus McKenzie at the

Blue Moon one night. But I learned my lesson. Never argue with a wolf."

As soon as the words were out, I wanted them back, all of them. *Oh shit. I'm too tired for this. I slipped up badly.*

He blinked at me, and an awkward silence stretched between us as his small black eyes searched my face.

I'd never wanted to tip my hand about how much I knew about the shifter community in New Fane. All I could do now was hope Officer Taylor misunderstood what I meant. But I wasn't counting on it. Not with the look on his face.

"Can you tell me what you mean by wolf?" Taylor took a step toward me, and I craned my neck to look up at him. "I think you need to explain exactly what you know about Mr. McKenzie."

"Besides that he's a dick who shifted in front of me and exposed your existence to me and tried to kill me for refusing to sleep with him?"

He blinked several times. "Jesus." There was suddenly a note of exasperation in his voice. Apparently, "Mr. McKenzie" had a reputation of his own. And apparently, the damned wolves of New Fane were more sympathetic toward their resident asshole than I had thought.

"Yeah. After that, I got a little paranoid and learned what I could about shifters and how to pick them out, because I half expected him to show up at my ranch or to send one of his friends. Fortunately, it seems like most shifters are better than that."

He just stared at me. He had put away his notebook. Understandably, he considered this part of the conversation to be off the record.

I squared my shoulders. "I know your partner is more than just a police officer. He's a bear-shifter, and a good one, though he needs to cover his tracks a little better. Shamus... Let's just say he's more of a rabid dog than he is wolf or human. But he's also an asshole, and I've learned to stay away."

For a long moment, we looked at each other, me trying to

stare him down from the distinct disadvantage point of being more than a foot shorter; him trying to do the same, but not succeeding. Finally, he took a breath and scowled.

"All right. But it's not something we want you talking about. Do you understand? It gets people nervous, and the last thing we want is frightened, trigger-happy folks going on a hunting trip."

I nodded. "Of course not. I don't want to make trouble for any of you, but I wasn't born yesterday, and a lady notices things. Especially after some prick attacks her in a parking lot and leaves her with reasons to be a little paranoid." I left it at that, not wanting to get into how I knew what I knew any more than I did how much I knew.

In reality, after my encounter with Shamus, I had scoured the Internet for rumors, and I had eventually found myself on a "monster hunter" forum that had sounded way too serious. I hadn't bought into their "all shifters are monsters" garbage, as I knew extremism when I saw it.

But I had played along. And I had learned a lot—only some of which was verifiable, but it had helped. I just never, ever wanted any shifter to know that I had been on those forums at all, any more than I wanted self-styled "shifter hunters" to know who or where I was.

"However, I really want you to tell me what your partner found behind my barn. He must have seen or smelled something." And I prayed that what he had uncovered involved no more shifters. They were a lot more dangerous than humans.

Taylor's frown deepened, but after a few moments of considering it, he nodded. "We're uncertain, but we think it's related to the break-in at Jack Mahony's last week."

"Oh shit. Jack? Really?" He wasn't a friend, but he was one of the better people around, and his job was one of the more necessary. Jack owned the county's only newspaper, and he lived above his office. I'd heard there had been a burglary, but nothing else. Jack had been more taciturn than usual when I'd last seen him in town, so I wasn't surprised he had said nothing. And now I knew why.

"What's the connection?" I could think of nothing that linked my ranch and Jack's newspaper. "I mean, it's not like we talk much. Not that he, you know, talks much at all to begin with." Especially for a guy who made his money on news and local gossip.

Now, I wondered if he was so withdrawn because he had been getting threats from some of the people he had exposed. And now, it seemed, one of them had made good on those threats. *Poor Jack.*

"We're pretty sure it's the mining and fracking groups that have been active lately, particularly the pro-fracking ones. They've gotten more vocal—and more aggressive—the more pushback they get from the community at large. Jack is against the strip-mining proposals on the table with local government and very vocal in his paper against fracking. Your father..."

"My father wrote the bill that would ban fracking altogether." My heart sank. *Shit.* This all came back to Dad. It always did. I should have guessed from the beginning that this involved one of his enemies.

Dammit, I just want to live my own life, out of his shadow.

"Yes. And he's been in the news lately. Jack published the senator's latest speech almost verbatim. The break-in happened shortly after that."

So, this guy thinks it's whoever is behind the push for fracking locally. And that I'm a target because of my father. "Did anyone shoot at Jack?"

Taylor shifted uneasily. "I don't believe so. Jack is a tough old bird, keeps to himself, but I think he'd have told me if someone had taken a potshot at him."

It made sense, although it made me sick to think this was all connected to something involving Dad. Corporations played dirty pool all the damned time, *but burning barns? Shooting at people—uninvolved people? Who the hell did this? I want to find that corporate asshole and force-feed him what's left of my barn.*

The phone rang downstairs, and I heard Henry's rumble as he answered. Taylor and I did an awkward two-step in the narrow hallway as he moved aside, and we headed back downstairs.

I stepped into the living room. Henry turned at the sound of my boots on the floor. And by the look on his face, I knew the call was more bad news.

"Yes, sir. Just a minute, sir." Henry met my eyes, and my heart dropped again. The only person Henry called sir was Dad.

I reached for the phone, and Henry handed it over as if it were a live rattler.

Dad's voice was already coming out of the phone before I got it to my ear. "I knew that irresponsible girl would end up in trouble out there at the ass-end of nowhere. Not only is she well away from anyplace secure, but she probably has drunk rednecks to deal with all the time. She should be here where I can monitor her."

"Dad?"

"Henry? Dammit, I said put her on the horn."

Oh, for fuck's sake. "Dad, stop ranting for a second and listen, all right? It's me."

He didn't even miss a beat, playing off his screw-up as if it hadn't happened. "About time, Alina. What the hell is happening out there? I had to hear from…my sources that someone burned down the house and tried to kill you. Why the hell didn't you call me?"

"Dad, it was the horse barn, not the house. And how did you even find out about all this? What sources do you have? Are you paying off one of my neighbors to spy on me now?" I closed my eyes and rubbed my forehead. Dad probably had the house wired or something equally intrusive. "If you've bugged my house or something. I'll go straight to the press."

"I do not have your house bugged," he said indignantly. "As

for the rest, you should be grateful that I care enough to monitor you."

"Grateful. That you're spying on me without my permission or, until now, my knowledge." I rolled my eyes and caught Henry smirking slightly as he turned to move away.

"If you weren't such a brat about everything and had stayed here where you belong..." he started.

"We're not having that argument again." He silenced immediately. Almost three decades of knowing each other, and he still reacted with shock whenever I stood up to him.

There was a warning in my tone that he couldn't have mistaken. His thirst for control of everyone around him was what had driven Mom away and had forced me to push him almost out of my life, though at least I still talked to him. Reluctantly, but I did. If he fucked around past a certain point, however, the last part of his family would shut him out completely, and he knew it.

He had loved Mom. He was just a total idiot about it—and borderline abusive. He remembered the loss. Talked about it a lot when he was drunk. Didn't want to go through it again. But here he was spying on me, and I had just caught him out.

He backed down with, "Fine. Just know that I have your best interests in mind."

I wanted to scream at him that my "best interests" weren't being considered if he was fucking spying on me. Not at all. But if I did that, it would open a whole can of worms, and poor Henry and Elizabeth—along with two cops—would end up a captive audience to a family fight. *That couldn't happen.* "We disagree."

"Back to someone shooting at you and burning your house down..." he said insistently.

I puffed out my cheeks briefly with exasperation. "It was the horse barn, not my house. The only thing that happened to my house was a broken window."

"From a bullet."

Only someone with access to my police report, or one of my own employees, would know that. I glanced around at a room full of suspects, dismissing Henry and Elizabeth right away. "Yes, that's right, and it sucks. But they missed, and the police are dealing with it."

"The police." He scoffed. "I'm not holding my breath for results from that small-town outfit."

"Even from the ones on your payroll?" I snapped before I could help myself.

He sucked air. *I was right.* But of course, he wouldn't admit it. He plowed on instead. "I want you on a plane home by tonight. It's only proper you spend Christmas with your family anyway."

"I'm thirty-three. You can't order me to do anything." I felt my blood pressure shoot up. Elizabeth and Henry had gone back to being interviewed by the two cops, but I could tell all four of them were hanging on every word I said during this low-key argument.

"I don't care how old you are. Get your butt on a plane tonight."

"No," I replied flatly.

"Now you're just being ridiculous. It would simplify everything..."

"It would simplify things for you. What it would do to me is drag me away from a pile of duties here, including boarding my horses and having my barn rebuilt. I'm also cooperating with the police on their investigation, something I can hardly do remotely."

Plus, I had no damn interest in going to another ridiculous Christmas party with a roomful of drunken, creepy politicians. *No. I promised myself I wouldn't do that ever again.*

"So, they don't want you to leave town?"

I exchanged glances with Taylor, who nodded at me. Apparently, his acute shifter hearing could make out everything Dad was saying. "No."

They weren't suspecting me of anything, I had finally realized. But I was also the victim in this case and an important witness.

"Fine, you win. Spend another Christmas alone on that worthless land you call a ranch."

"Thanks for your permission," I snarled.

His stupid parties, like his yearly demands, had killed my Christmas spirit. It now boiled down to breakfast with my staff and an exchange of gifts with them and a few friends.

No parties.

No caroling.

No Christmas dinner.

And especially no mistletoe.

"I'm sending someone from DC to watch over you," Dad answered. "You're incapable of taking care of yourself." His disdain for me and my need for independence dripped from his every word.

"Bullshit. I can take care of myself. You're not sending anyone here." My father's ego and meddling in my life made me feel like an angry teenager again, struggling against someone who would always, insistently, see me as an incompetent child whose life should be watched and controlled for my own good.

Henry dropped his eyes and turned away.

Officer Taylor stood in the doorway, still listening with obvious interest. I scowled at him, but it didn't seem to make a dent in his tough-guy exterior.

Dad was chattering on like nothing that I said made a dent in him either. "You can't stay there with no kind of protection. It's not safe. I'm sure you've been sniffing around already, so you know about the news reporter and what happened to him. Those crazy loonies with the fracking coalition are dangerous. You need protection."

I rolled my eyes. "It's being handled already. And crazy loonies is redundant, Dad."

"Don't get smart with me, young lady." He was sputtering.

I could imagine Dad, sitting behind his enormous mahogany

desk, some aide or administrative assistant cringing at his side, waiting for instructions. He got his way through intimidation and sheer force of will.

And while I thoroughly resented his tactics with me, and my life, I had a grudging admiration for his track record on Capitol Hill. At least there, he was trying to do good for the folks back home in Montana, even if he looked down his nose at most of the residents for being "country."

But whenever his focus narrowed to just one resident of the state—me—I completely lost it. I couldn't stand his urge to control everyone close to him, according to him, "for our own good." He was also disrespectful of everyone else's intelligence and ability, especially mine.

"I'm not getting smart," I responded. "I'm telling you I don't need you to protect me or to send someone to protect me. I can take care of myself. And I already have some help anyway."

"It's not negotiable, young lady. Someone will be there tonight." The tone of his voice told me he'd probably already given someone orders to pack up and leave tonight, eliminating any chance of them having Christmas with their family.

"Dad. Stop. Listen to me." My voice had gotten louder, taken on that nasty edge only Dad could bring out in me. I took a breath, looking up at nosy-ass Officer Taylor. I wished he'd just go away. But he stayed where he was, as solid as the mountains outside.

Dad went on, giving me the same lecture he always did.

"No. Not this time. I listened when you left law school and bought that worthless piece of property. I listened when you ended your engagement to Charles. I listened when…"

Why the hell did he always have to bring up Charles?

Charles was my last serious relationship. After him, I kept men at arm's length. Charles had been one reason I had left Washington. He was a lobbyist instead of a politician. Dad had adored him and pushed me to keep the engagement, even after I had caught the bastard in bed with another woman. Dad had never forgiven me for refusing his "kind advice" and taking off instead.

"I've heard this before, Dad. I've put up with it because I know you mean well, even if you do not understand what a personal boundary is. But this time, it's different. I'm not letting you send someone to babysit me."

"Ma'am?" Officer Taylor stepped forward.

"What?" I glared up at him. "Just a minute, Dad." I put my hand over the receiver, cutting off my dad's grating voice. He was already starting to repeat himself in his lectures, trying to draw me into the old fight again. I didn't want to hear it anyway.

Taylor cleared his throat. "Tell your father I have someone who can do what he asks. Someone more qualified."

"I don't want anyone, qualified or not, babysitting me," I countered.

"You need someone, because you're currently under threat. You need added security. And I think who I have in mind would be a better choice than someone from DC."

I blew out a breath. "Fine." At least it would keep Dad from controlling my life through some sunglasses-and-earbuds type he'd dug up from his staff. I took my hand away from the phone. "Dad, the police are here, and they have someone local who's qualified to do whatever it is you think needs doing."

There was silence on the other end, a welcome moment of peace. Then Dad surprised me. "Let me talk to him."

I handed the phone to Officer Taylor. He listened for a moment and then responded with a series of "Yes, sirs" and "No, sirs." I could just imagine the questions being peppered at him by Dad.

"The two of them are former military, plus ten years at a private security firm," Taylor stated, then waited a few moments. "No, sir. They are now partners in their own executive security firm. They specialize in celebrity security, VIP protection, and bodyguard services for high-net-worth individuals. They have an unblemished record of success protecting the client's safety, confidentiality, and peace of mind. And they owe me a favor, so they'll take this job."

Now, I was interested. Two bodyguards, with way better credentials than some wet-behind-the-ears city kid who had only been on the job for a year or two. I knew Dad would not spare any of his more senior security staff, even for me.

During Taylor's conversation with Dad, he was a rock, unfailingly polite but not intimidated at all. I could only imagine how frustrating that was for Dad, who hated it enough when I didn't defer. *But a stranger?* I was sure that only the cop's calm professionalism kept dear old Dad from exploding.

"No, sir. We'll be posting a squad car at the gate until they get here, as a deterrent in case those crazies circle back and cause more trouble."

I opened my mouth to protest, but at least out by the gate wouldn't invade my privacy. I closed it again and just listened to the bear-shifter stand up to Dad in a polite but implacable way I only wished I could imitate.

He went back to the "Yes, sir-No, sir," game for a while and gave a few more details: "Yes, they're bonded." "Yes, they have strong ties to law enforcement, both here and in Billings, where they run their business." "No, they definitely aren't anti-environmentalist or vote conservative, as far as I know."

Finally, Taylor hung up. I thought he looked a little drained. But I was glad he had ended the call without letting Dad get in any more digs at me or bark any more orders.

"Your father has decided not to send anyone and to let me handle it from this end. For now anyway. I imagine he'll be calling you to check in." He glanced at Henry and Elizabeth, standing in the corner, quiet as church mice. Like me, they had probably been waiting for my dad's explosion, but something in Taylor's answers had somehow satisfied Dad. Taylor motioned for me to follow him into the small room I used as my office, closing the door behind him.

"Here's the deal," Taylor started. "I have a couple of friends who deal in this kind of situation." He scratched his beard stubble, already sporting beyond a five-o'clock shadow in the early afternoon.

"Well, that's lucky, I guess. Not sure how you talked my dad into it. So, you said they're in security?"

"Yes, and they're excellent at what they do."

I folded my arms. At least this would prevent Dad from trying to take control of my life...again. "Do you really think this whole situation is that serious?"

Taylor's expression went grave. "I do. I suspect this fracking group is escalating in its aggression. I think they're behind this, and not just because of last night or the mess with the newspaper. What your father didn't tell you is that there have been threats made against him."

"What?" *Why the hell didn't Dad say anything?* Was he trying to seem invincible to me? I shook my head with dismay. Dad's pride was as big as Montana. "So, this has gone well beyond just local groups, then." Either that or they were traveling around the country to target people, which didn't sound right. Especially when one of those people was a local journalist, and the other was a senator's estranged daughter.

"We think so. It was one thing that your father made very clear to me. He suspects so too. But getting back to you and who I'd like to send out here. You need to know something about them."

"Yes?"

He cleared his throat. "They're shifters."

I shook my head. "And why am I not surprised by this?"

Office Taylor frowned. "You have something against shifters?"

"I'm not against your people. Just the one asshole." I tilted my head curiously as his lips quirked slightly. "And I guess every group has those."

"Yeah, fair enough." He shrugged his massive shoulders. "And

I will not lie—we shifters have our share of assholes. That guy you stood up to is pretty infamous."

"I'm not surprised. So, these security guys, they'll come here and watch the ranch?" I didn't know how my animals would react to a bunch of shifters. It worried me they would smell "large predators" on the men and become skittish.

Taylor shook his head. "No. You'll go somewhere safe until we find whoever is after you. It's too dangerous to leave you here."

I held up my hands, shaking my head. "No. I'm not leaving. I'm staying right here. This is my land and my animals. I have a duty to both." And I wasn't giving up either, not even temporarily.

Taylor folded his arms and stared at me.

I stared right back, which seemed to surprise him. I was pretty sure there weren't many people who disagreed with him. But I wasn't leaving my ranch, and I wasn't leaving Henry alone.

"What about Henry?" I asked. "He lives here too, along with his family." Of course, their cottage was acres away, on the far side of the property, to give us all some proper space. "If I leave with the extra security, he'd be a sitting duck, tough or not."

Henry would have rolled his eyes if he had overheard me worrying. But it wasn't like I was wrong. If I needed protection, so did he.

Officer Taylor nodded and ran a hand through his hair. "We'll plan for someone to stay with him, to help look after the ranch."

I leaned against the edge of my desk, trying to wrap my mind around everything that had happened. Someone wanted me dead because of who my father was. I couldn't change that. It was out of my control. And that also meant I couldn't change the fact that I needed extra protection right now. Officer Taylor was right. I still wanted to rebel. I had fought hard for the right to live my own life. But I had Henry and Elizabeth to think of. If I was at risk, so were they. Elizabeth, I could send back into town to her home. She deserved some time off for Christmas anyway.

But Henry would be here, keeping watch alone, and his family would be here too, possibly in the line of fire as well if something bad went down.

No way was I letting that happen.

Christ, I really can't deal with this right now.

My stomach was in knots, and a dull throbbing headache had started behind my eyes. I was running on no sleep and little food. I was sick and tired of this whole clusterfuck. "Why are you so invested in getting me my own bodyguards?"

"I don't need your father sending some human here who might stumble on to the fact that we have a hell of a lot of shifters living in this area. We'd like to keep our kind off the Washington, DC, radar."

His rationale, I understood. The government would love to find shifters to experiment on. "I give in," I stated. "You can call your shifter friends. What type of shifters are they? Bears like you?"

Taylor shook his head, flashing me a wry grin. "Wolves, but they're not assholes."

After the shitty impression that last wolf-shifter made, I was wary of his kind. But in this situation, beggars couldn't be choosers. "Fine. As long as they don't get too overbearing." *Like the last one,* I didn't have to add.

He was already nodding. "That won't be a problem. These two know how to mind their manners."

We walked back into the living room. Henry and Elizabeth both looked up at me expectantly.

I cleared my throat. "Here's where we are with this situation. Someone tried to" —*I couldn't say kill*— "hurt me. Probably the same person who burned down the horse barn. It's not safe for me to be here. Officer Taylor is going to have someone come and take me somewhere safe." I looked at Henry. "He's sending someone to stay here and help look after the ranch."

Henry was already rising, shaking his head. I held up my hand, and he settled uneasily back onto the couch.

"Henry, this is way beyond a rogue bear or a pissed-off neighbor. The people behind this are violent fanatics. They burglarized the local newspaper and have threatened its proprietor. They tried to snipe me through my window, and we don't even know how many there are. They are threatening not just me, but my dad, and they will not stop until someone stops them. This is serious."

Elizabeth looked as numb as I felt, but Henry was still in fight rather than flight mode.

Henry scowled. "I don't need anyone babysitting me. I can run this place, finish the lambing and get the horses boarded on my own."

I sat down beside him and took his hand. He looked from my face to our hands and back, and he relaxed a little. "Henry, listen. I don't want this any more than you do. But it's out of our hands. If this weren't necessary, I wouldn't have agreed to it." I looked pleadingly into his eyes, trying to convey how desperate this situation was. "They tried to take me out with a rifle. There's nothing stopping them from trying to do the same to you or your family, and I can't stand that idea. Let us give you some backup."

He stared at me for a few moments, then shook his head. "If you say so, Miss Glory. Only because *you* say so." Henry squeezed my hand, and I almost cried.

Why does everything in my life have to get upended because of who fathered me?

And will Taylor's wolf-shifter friends be able to protect me?

4

"Alina, there's someone here for you." Elizabeth's voice floated up the stairs. She sounded odd, breathless.

Oh God, what now?

It had been three chaotic days since the fire. There were too many visitors—cops, claims adjusters from the insurance company, curious neighbors, even a reporter. Not to mention, all the unpleasant surprises. The deductible for replacing the barn. Questions about arson. That no one within driving distance seemed to have room for my horses, and Storm, especially, was getting sick of his cramped quarters in the sheep barn. I did not understand what was about to confront me downstairs, and I didn't want to face it. But I wouldn't get anywhere hiding from my problems, and the urgency in Elizabeth's voice really got my attention.

I quickly rinsed the toothpaste from my mouth and ran down the stairs. Turning the corner full speed at the bottom, I almost collided with a man standing in the hallway. *Damn, that's twice this week. I need to take that corner slower.*

"Oh crap, sorry! I..." My voice died as I stared up into a pair of the bluest eyes I'd ever seen.

I was not easily taken in by gorgeous men, but I looked up at him speechlessly. Dazzling blue eyes with long, boyish lashes, set in a broad, handsome face, and a devilishly charming smile. I had to remember to blink...and breathe.

He didn't blink, which gave me a clue who I was dealing with. *He's a shifter. He has to be one of the wolf-shifters here to protect me.*

Beyond him, I could see Elizabeth standing by the open door, staring at his back like she'd just met a movie star. I could hardly blame her.

The man standing in my hallway was beyond handsome. He had thick, white-blond hair that was swept back from a high forehead, strong, rugged features, a wide, well-shaped mouth. He had to be the hottest guy I had ever met, even dressed down.

He smiled faintly as I stared up at him. "Ms. Glory?"

"Yeah... Yes. I am. Hi." *Holy shit, girl, get it together.* But that was a tall order in the face of all this hotness.

He extended a hand, and I reached out automatically, shaking it. "It's a pleasure to meet you. I'm Tucker Fernsby. I believe you were expecting me."

His handshake was firm but not crushing. There was a long moment where he held my hand and my gaze...and all of my attention. Then he let my hand go, and I felt as if he'd both taken something away and left something behind. I made a soft fist, wanting to hold on to the warmth of his touch.

"Nice to meet you too. Follow me." I turned back to the living room and caught Elizabeth still lurking in the doorway. She gave me a flustered smile, ducking out of sight. "Please, Mr. Fernsby. Have a seat." I sat in the armchair beside the couch. The man sat across from me in the other armchair, seemingly far more comfortable than I was. He crossed one leg over the other, ankle resting on his knee. I noticed he was wearing an expensive pair of cowboy boots, worn but cared for, nicely made.

"Can I get you anything? Coffee? Water?" I suddenly wanted a stiff drink, but it was far too early.

"No, thank you. I think I should just lay out our basic plan, see if you have questions, and then get on the road."

His words hit the brakes on my distraction, as pleasant as it was. I had been thinking all night about how I didn't want to leave my ranch. It had bothered me enough that I had changed my mind. I was going to challenge the idea, even if I lost. I wasn't leaving my home without a fight.

"Yes. About that. I'm not going anywhere." I kept my smile on as his faded.

"Is that so?" He lifted an eyebrow, sounding just slightly annoyed.

"Yes. This is my life, and I'm needed here. You can just stay here, monitor things..." My voice trailed off under his gaze. There was something hard and unyielding in those blue eyes.

"I'm sorry if that's what they have led you to believe, Ms. Glory. It's my plan to take you away from where the danger is, not leave you in the middle of it."

I sighed in exasperation. "Look, Mr. Fernsby—"

"Tucker, please." He leaned back, one long arm stretched across the back of the couch. The muscles in his arm strained the fabric of his crisp white shirt. "We're going to be in close quarters, and I'd like us to be at least on a first-name basis."

"Well, Tucker, I don't want to be a pain in the ass, but I'm not leaving my ranch or my people. This is lambing season. I'm needed here. And I don't feel like letting some bastards who are actually after my father scare me away from my home. So, how are we going to come to an agreement?"

The corners of his mouth tightened in what wasn't quite a smile. "May I call you Alina?"

"Sure."

"Okay, Alina." He leaned forward, elbows resting on his knees, hands loosely clasped. "Here's how this is going to work." His voice had gotten softer, and I leaned forward despite myself.

"You're going to go pack a bag, just the essentials. Then we're going to get into my SUV, and we're going someplace secure.

And we're going to stay there until someone contacts me to tell me it's safe to bring you back here. You understand?"

I blinked, sitting back. *He might have my safety in mind, but he does not give the orders around here.*

I kept my voice calm. "Mr. Fernsby…Tucker. I understand you're here for my welfare. And believe me, I appreciate it. But this wasn't my idea. It was my father's, who would rather bark orders at me than treat me like an equal adult." I put a little emphasis on that last bit. "A local cop you know worked out a compromise, but both of them forgot to include me in that discussion. I'm really not into letting anyone else, especially men I barely know, make my life decisions for me. I'm still not sure it's even necessary for me to leave my home."

He sighed heavily. "Your life—and that of anyone in your employment—is in danger. So, would you like to reconsider your stance on leaving the ranch?"

Wolves. I did not understand if all of them had alpha-asshole disease, but this one clearly had a case of it.

Tucker sat back, waiting. His expression wasn't a patient one, and he still kept trying to stare me down.

I thought about the fire, the terror and panic of that night, and the bullet hole in my bedroom wall.

"Fine. It's reconsidered, but here's the alternate plan. I'll pack, and then we're going to take the horses and ride up into the mountains. There's a cabin up there that I own. It's well stocked and safe. It's also no place anyone would ever go, except me. Henry—my ranch foreperson—is the only one who knows where it is. And you can't even take a car up there. So, we go there, and when this all ends, we'll come back down."

Tucker tipped his head to the side, a faint smile on his face. I waited for him to shoot down my plan. The silence stretched on for a few minutes as he digested my counteroffer. Finally, he exhaled a long breath.

"I can tell you're used to getting your way, Alina, even when powerful men are trying to get you to do otherwise. And I'm sure it's why you're out here, on a ranch in a remote part of Montana, instead of in Washington with your father."

My hackles went up. "If you're implying that I'm difficult to get along with—"

He raised one hand and one eyebrow. "I'm not implying anything. I'm stating a fact. If you're uncomfortable with that, or think it implies anything, that's your problem."

Oh, for fuck's sake. If I could, I'd have shown him out of the house, but then there would be hell to pay on all fronts. *Dammit. Okay, fine. I'll just calm down, hear him out, and hope he has a good reason for his attitude.*

For the first time in a long while, I bit my tongue, seething as Tucker continued, "Don't take it as an insult. If someone told me I was headstrong and opinionated, I'd agree on all counts." He leaned back again, giving all the appearance that he was having a normal conversation. But this was far from normal. For me, anyway. Maybe he was used to giving orders at work or with his pack, but I wasn't used to taking them.

"Okay. So, let's agree to disagree about where you want to take me, or how headstrong, bullheaded, and opinionated I am. This is what it is. You're a total stranger who talks to me in ways I don't even tolerate from my own father. And apparently, you think anyone who stands up to you is just being stubborn and doesn't have any kind of filter. So, I'll just repeat myself until you get it. I'm not going anywhere except to the cabin. You have a choice. You can stay here, or you can come with me."

I stood up, and from this angle, I could stare him down. At least until he unfolded himself from the couch and rose.

He took a step toward me, and my first instinct was to back away. But I held my ground. He was a lot like Storm. If he got it in his head that he could intimidate me, I'd end up being trampled. And I wasn't about to lie down and let him do it.

The room was quiet, and I could hear the ticking of the mantel clock and Elizabeth's footsteps in the kitchen.

Nothing in Tucker's expression gave away what was going on

in his head, but I had a good idea he had just as many thoughts as were swirling around in mine. I waited for whatever conclusion he'd come to. As long as he didn't throw his weight around physically, I figured I could handle it.

It surprised me when he smiled, a genuine smile that crinkled the corners of his eyes. He was pleased that I had pushed back? *Interesting.*

"You'd make an excellent politician. Maybe it's in the blood. We'll go where you want, on the condition that we do everything else the way *I* want. Believe me when I say that it's for your own good. Because if I'm giving orders, it's because your safety is at risk and you need to act promptly. No arguments, disagreements, or disobedience. No temper tantrums either. We don't have the time or the patience."

"I don't throw tantrums. I stand up for myself."

He laughed. I didn't think there was anything to laugh about. With a sinking feeling, I realized I might have won the battle but lost the war. We'd go to my cabin, but I'd be under his thumb the entire time, under the guise of him looking after my safety.

"I'm assuming the cabin has supplies for both us and the horses for a few weeks?" he asked. "You said it's well stocked. You don't strike me as a woman who would head off someplace unless there were more provisions waiting at the other end than some apples and a bottle of wine."

I didn't like that he could read me so easily. But at least some of his opinions were favorable and on the nose. "It has the basics. There's a well, propane, firewood, and a fully equipped place for the horses. The cupboard's stocked with canned food, coffee, flour, all the basics. There's also a propane chest freezer full of food. Depending on how long we stay...we should be fine."

That seemed to satisfy him, and he nodded. "Go pack. I want to talk to your foreperson. What's his name?"

"Henry. He's probably in the sheep barn right now. Out across the yard, in the building with the green metal door." It was the only larger building that was still standing besides the house, but I didn't want to mention the burned barn, even in passing. It still stung.

"Got it." He turned and let himself out of the house. I watched him through the front windows as he strode across the yard. He moved with a controlled energy, a power that I'd sensed in the house but was very obvious as he walked to the barn. He opened the door and looked inside. Henry must have been there because Tucker disappeared inside, pulling the door shut behind him.

I turned away and went up to my room to pack. For a minute, I focused on grabbing what I thought I'd need, what was essential. At least that was something I had a modicum of control over.

But the welter of conflicting emotions inside me rose, and I sat on the bed, holding a shirt. I looked out the window over the field to the woods. I had boarded up the broken pane, and briefly, I wondered if there was someone out there with a high-powered rifle sight trained on me through the other windows. Fear ran through me. I'd been sleeping in the downstairs guest room since the fire, as if tossing and fighting with my pillow counted as sleep. I'd contemplated sleeping in the sheep barn and braving the freezing temperatures out there whenever I had to run back to the house. There were no windows big or low enough to shoot at me through, and I literally could have counted sheep until I fell asleep.

Again, I got that terrible sense that things had spun out of control. I kept coming back to that word—*control*. I'd lost it almost completely over the last seventy-two hours, and that was a distinctly unsettling feeling. I'd lost it first by being Dad's daughter. I'd been helpless as the barn burned. Someone had taken advantage of that and shot through my window. It was only because of the lambing that I'd been on the couch instead of in my bed. Only dumb luck had saved me, not anything I had done for myself.

And now I was saddled with this protector, this man—wolf-shifter—who, from what'd I'd been told, was here to look out for me. He had come in barking orders, and when I pushed back, he seemed alternately patronizing and amused by me. I didn't like that. This differed from giving me instructions for my safety. He was looking down on me. He wasn't my superior, and he needed to stop acting that way. But he just wouldn't, and it was pissing me off.

He'd gotten his way, even though we were going to the cabin. It felt almost as if they had tricked me into giving in to his plans to move by fighting for what I wanted. I didn't like that feeling either. I was still leaving my home, even if I had gotten him to alter some terms. It bothered me that I had almost automatically sought a compromise instead of standing my ground.

And most irritating of all was the fact that, despite all the negatives, all the things I didn't like about Tucker Fernsby, I was attracted to him. I didn't want to feel any of this, and I chalked it up to poor judgment because of stress and lack of sleep.

The front door slammed downstairs, and I heard Henry's deep rumble, counterpoint to Tucker's more mellow tones, as their boots clumped across my floor. Elizabeth's laughter floated up to my room, and I rose from my seat on my bed, stuffing the shirt I had been holding into my pack. Dragging my feet would not make any of this go away.

After hastily packing a few more outfits, I grabbed my bag and went downstairs. Henry and Tucker were standing by the fireplace; Elizabeth was back in the kitchen. I caught Henry's eye, and he excused himself from his conversation with Tucker to come talk to me.

"Are you going to be okay here?" I asked Henry. "Until the other guy shows up?" Henry was tough and capable, but I was worried, and I couldn't hide it. This mess had worn all of us down. And besides, he had a family back at his cottage. They could end up targets, too.

Henry scrubbed a hand across his face. For the first time in what seemed like ages, I really looked at him, saw the deep lines in his face, the rough stubble on his cheeks. He looked as exhausted as I felt.

"I'll be okay. He said that my backup will be here in an hour. The general plan is to hunker down, keep watch, take care of ranch business, and let the police do their work." He scratched his cheek. "You're going to have to leave me some guidance as to how much freedom they have to search the place."

I nodded. "I can't even keep them out of my bedroom at this point since someone put a bullet through my window. I'm really sorry you're caught up in this, Henry."

He shrugged. "We've been through a lot together, Miss Glory. We'll get through this too."

Tears welled up in my eyes, and I brushed them away. "Okay, then. I've got my cell, and I'll get the satellite dish to connect us to the net as soon as we hike up there. Call, even if you think it's nothing, even if the other guy thinks it's nothing. I don't care if the only thing that happens is another lamb born. I want to know about it."

Henry set one big, work-hardened hand on my shoulder. "I'll be okay. I'll watch out for the ranch. You watch out for yourself." He jerked his head over his shoulder. "That guy seems to know what he's doing. Makes me feel a little better about you going off with him."

There was more unsaid in his words, and I wondered what their conversation in the barn had been. I wasn't sure if he was trying to reassure me—or himself. But I couldn't even get started on my first question about his barn conversation before Tucker was suddenly at my elbow.

"We need to get going," Tucker rumbled. "There is actually some urgency here, whether you want to believe that."

I glared at him. But he was right, even if I hated to admit it. "I'm ready. But are you?" Hands on hips, I looked him up and down. "Can you ride?" I had the image of him trying to load a suitcase on a horse.

"I'll manage." The self-assured look on his face pricked my curiosity. "Let's go."

I grabbed my bag before he could, and we headed out to the tack shed. Tucker detoured to his vehicle, reaching in to grab a battered leather bag out of the back.

"You've ridden before?" I fell into step beside him.

"Yes." Tucker walked easily across the yard, looking like he was heading out for a pleasure ride. But he was anything but relaxed. His gaze moved across the yard, down the fence line, to the woods, taking in everything. He was on alert, tensed.

I thanked whatever entity had guided whoever built Stone's Throw in such a haphazard way, and that its rolling landscape kept me from making too many changes. The fire had destroyed the barn and the hay in the loft. But the tack room was in a separate building, a metal shed set away from the barn that had survived the fire with minimal damage. In the past, I'd cursed the fact that it was inconvenient, but now it proved to be a godsend.

I pulled open the door, flipping on the light. The smell of leather and horse and saddle soap washed over me, and I took a moment to stand, breathing it all in, reminded of past happiness. But anger and sadness welled up again. I was sick of having my life upended, but here I was, dealing with another disruption.

But where would I be if I caved in to Dad's wishes and went back to that placid, boring, completely stifled life as a senator's daughter in Washington? I could feel my chest tighten just thinking about it. *No. Freedom here is worth the risks.* But it was time to think in survival mode. Time to take control of my life again, if only by working to protect it and what was important to me.

Elizabeth had already left. I had told her to go home, to stay away until someone let her know it was safe to return. The guys could cook for themselves. Though I wished I knew more about Henry's backup, as he would live in my house for the duration. "Tell me again who's taking care of Henry and the ranch?"

"I have someone who's going to come out to watch the place. Henry will be fine. The ranch will be fine."

That wasn't good enough. "Who is he? Another shifter?"

For the first time, Tucker looked surprised.

I stared back at him. "I know what you are, Mr. Tucker Fernsby. Your bear buddies told me when they found out I'm knowledgeable about shifters."

He held my gaze for a long moment before nodding slowly. "I suppose that makes sense given what they told me. And yes, the man coming to the ranch is a shifter." He rubbed his nose and looked almost uncomfortable. "There's something else you need to know."

Somehow, that didn't surprise me. "And what would that be?"

But before he could answer, a massive white SUV turned into the drive. It pulled up, and I watched as a tall, sophisticated-looking man stepped out, wearing dark pants and a well-cut wool coat. I assumed he was a particularly well-dressed insurance adjuster. But he wasn't looking at me; he was looking at the man standing beside me.

"Tucker," the man greeted.

"You're late," Tucker grumbled in response as he shut the door behind the newcomer.

"Yes, well, I got stuck behind a semi for half the trip. How is it going?" He gave me a once-over and a calm smile. It was as charming as Tucker's, but more low-key.

"We're ready to go, pretty much. Slight change of venue, but it might be a better spot for her than taking her back to Billings."

I turned to Tucker as the newcomer nodded. "This is your surprise?"

Tucker managed a smile. "Alina Glory, let me introduce Axel Marks. My partner."

Axel Marks held out his hand. I looked from him to Tucker and back again and then shook his hand. His grip was firm and warm like Tucker's, and his gaze was as steady. It put me that much more off-balance, which I hated. At least he was also just as easy on the eyes.

"You didn't tell her, did you?" Axel turned to Tucker with a wry smile. "You never do."

"Partner? You're a couple?" I couldn't really see them as a couple. Both were the dominant type, and all that butting heads seemed like it would ruin anything romantic. They also couldn't be more different in looks. Where Tucker was rugged and carried the scent of the outdoors, Axel was chiseled, refined, like he'd stepped out of the pages of *GQ* magazine. The juxtaposition of the two men was startling, and the thought of them as a couple blew my mind.

Tucker's bemused expression almost made me laugh. "Hell no. Axel's my business partner." He waved his hand between us. "He's coming with us up the mountain."

Both Axel and I stared at Tucker, but it was obviously for very different reasons.

"What mountain?" Axel's brows drew together, his dark eyes

growing even darker. The intensity in his expression only played up his brooding good looks. Tucker seemed like the sort who would talk you into bed. Despite his polished appearance, Axel seemed like the sort who would just carry you there.

Tucker held up his hand. "There's been a change in plans. A compromise of sorts. We're taking her to a remote location in the mountains."

I raised an eyebrow in Tucker's direction. That was the closest he'd come to admitting he'd given some ground in this whole bizarre experience.

Axel frowned as he processed this, then offered a charming smile. "Well then, I guess I should get my stuff. And change clothes since I can hardly ride in a suit. We're heading out now?"

"We were just going to saddle the horses. Lucky for you, I have three of them." I headed back into the tack barn. Axel strode off toward his vehicle, leaving me with Tucker.

"Those two, and the rest are over there." I pointed to the saddles for Storm and Mary. I grabbed Jane's tack, and we brought all of it out to the yard.

"It must have been hard, having the barn go." Tucker stood, looking at the charred ruins of the barn.

I dropped what I was carrying and straightened. I'd avoided looking at the rubble, walking with my head down between the buildings. But now, I followed Tucker's gaze. Blackened wood jutted up, outlined against the sky, still looking like the ribs of some strange beast.

"It tore out my heart. At least we got the horses out, but it's a tremendous loss." The only good thing about having to take the horses up the mountain was that I wouldn't have to board them. Not that I had found any boarding space since the fire, to begin with.

"I am sorry, Alina."

I found Tucker's arm around my shoulders. Besides Henry, it was the first hug I'd had since the barn fire, since I'd realized someone had tried to shoot me. Even though it was Tucker, and his gesture surprised me, I realized I wanted comfort. I let him pull me against him, resting my head on his shoulder, turning my face into his jacket. It felt fantastic. He even smelled good. I did my best to ignore that, but it was impossible. In the back of my head, I wondered why I had caved in to his embrace so easily. Maybe I needed comfort that badly. Or maybe something within me trusted him more than I did consciously.

"Thank you." We stood for a moment, and I closed my eyes, inhaling the scent of this strange man. He was warm and smelled of fresh air, and impossibly, of all things, Balkan pipe tobacco. My granddad had smoked Balkan, and a sudden memory of sitting on his lap, drowsily listening to him read me a bedtime story as I watched his pipe tobacco wreathing his head, rose in my mind. Unexpected tears welled up, and I pulled away, swiping a hand across my eyes.

He tilted his head slightly, openly concerned. "You okay? I didn't mean to upset you."

I shook my head. "I'm just tired. It's been a long few days." Abruptly, I turned and walked to the sheep shed, yanking open the door. Fiona looked up, her four small, curved horns catching the faint light. She stomped a foot in agitation, her lambs scut-tling behind her. She should have been out in the pasture, but I wanted her to be safe indoors with the other new moms. It was irrational, but I couldn't turn her out yet.

The horses snorted. Even though they were stuck in the smaller quarters of the sheep barn, I'd been reluctant to let them out as much. It seemed a little cruel, but I did it because I didn't want them used as target practice if the shooter couldn't find me to aim at.

"Cute little thing. Feisty. She's a Jacob?"

I turned, surprised to find Axel standing in the doorway, dressed in jeans now and a faded denim jacket with a sheepskin lining. Behind him, I saw a leather bag, not too dissimilar to Tucker's.

"Yes. You have an expert eye. She's a purebred." I nodded to the lambs peeking out at us. "Buck and ewe, born earlier this week. Also purebred. First of the stock I hope to increase."

Axel leaned on the edge of the stall while Tucker stood silently beside me. I stood between them, and for a minute, we watched Fiona and the as-yet-unnamed lambs. I wanted to stay here. I didn't want to leave my home.

"Listen, guys. Really. Are you sure...?"

"Yes." Tucker turned to me. "Yes, I'm sorry, but it is necessary. It's not just a matter of what I want. And we need to go. Now."

I sighed, turning toward the horses, and opened the stalls.

I pointed to Tucker, then to the big black horse. "You can ride Storm. He can be a handful, though, so be careful." I would have preferred to ride him, but Mary was too small for either of these two gigantic men. Jane was taller and stronger and could handle one of them.

Tucker stepped into the stall and reached for Storm's bridle. The horse tossed his head, whites of his eyes showing. I took a step back, expecting the worst.

But Tucker murmured something, and Storm's snorts and head-tossing subsided. I watched in amazement as he reached up and stroked the big horse's neck. "Easy there, friend. I'm here with your mistress." He patted Storm, calming him further.

There was something powerful about a man who could calm a strong and potentially dangerous creature through sounds and touch alone. Maybe I'd misjudged Tucker. Maybe he wasn't the jerk I had thought he was.

I heard a chuckle beside me. "That's my partner. He's full of surprises."

Axel was watching me stare at Tucker. My face grew hot, and I turned away, reaching for the latch on Mary's stall, stepping inside and away from Axel's piercing gaze. I felt like they had caught me with my hand in the cookie jar, and it made me angry with myself. *Get your shit together. Your emotions are all over the place, and it won't make a good impression.* And though I didn't completely know why, I wanted to impress these guys.

Axel's smile said he knew exactly what I was thinking, and I didn't like that at all. I glanced back, caught his quirked eyebrow, and he finally had the good grace to turn away.

"I'll take this one. She looks like my kind of girl." He stepped into Jane's stall, coming up from the rear. The tall, black-and-white filly looked back at him as if he were the devil incarnate, and before I could voice a warning, she swung around and banged him against the wall with her flank. "Apparently the feeling is not mutual."

I couldn't help but laugh as he backed away. I knew she'd never kick, but she could tell you exactly what she thought with her body language. "You came up behind her, and you smell like a predator. Give her a chance to get a good look at you."

"I thought you said the stallion was the handful." Axel gave me a reproachful look, giving Jane a wide berth as he moved farther into her field of vision.

I wiped my eyes. "Well, she doesn't know you, and she doesn't know what tobacco smells like." Nobody who worked with her regularly smoked. "Or shifters."

Axel didn't look surprised that I'd brought it up. Either someone had briefed him, or he had the best poker face I had ever seen. "Okay then, any other advice? It's been a few years, and the horses I worked with before were shifter-raised."

"Just be calm and assertive. She'll cooperate once you show her that you're in charge and that you won't hurt her." I leaned on the stall door, watching the two of them dancing around each other in the small space. Jane's ears weren't flat, but she snorted and kept shifting to monitor him at all times.

"She's not like your other conquests, Axel. She's got more sense." Tucker's tone was teasing and a little smug. He had Storm by the halter, leading him out of the barn.

Axel shot him a look and turned back to Jane. He reached for her, got her by the halter, and gave a firm tug. She snorted, but she settled down, gave him one last look, and followed him out of the stall.

I patted Mary on the neck, took her bridle, and brought up the end of the line. As I walked, the image of Axel's confident smile temporarily crumpling as he got bounced off the stall wall had me working my mouth to keep from snickering. *Not perfect. But at least he has a sense of humor about it.* I suspected I would have an easier time getting along with him than Tucker, even if he seemed thoroughly citified.

The men knew their way around the tack. It impressed me how quickly they saddled their mounts. We were just finishing up when a truck pulled into the yard.

Tucker handed me Storm's reins. "Damn, finally. That's Benny. I'd hoped he'd show up before we took off. He'll be staying here until it's safe to come back. I'll take him into the house and introduce him to Henry. Thought we might have to leave a note."

A heavyset blond man wearing a baseball hat got out of the truck. He and Tucker exchanged a few words, and then they disappeared into the house.

I glanced over. Axel was stroking Jane's neck, looking like he was ready for a ride around the ranch, but just like Tucker, he was scanning the woods, watching a car going by on the road. His posture held the same contained energy Tucker exhibited. I didn't know if it was a security-guy thing, a military-guy thing, or a wolf-shifter thing.

I tried to make conversation to break the tension. "Have you been working together long?"

Axel turned his gaze to me. I noticed lines at the corners of his eyes, the kind someone got from being outdoors, from squinting in the sun. He didn't strike me as the outdoors type, but I was questioning my perceptions of almost everything—and everyone—lately. Especially these two. *Who are these men I'm now depending on for my safety?*

"We met years ago, after our tours overseas ended. We

worked for an agency that coordinated men like us to deal with situations like this."

I winced. I didn't like the reminder I was in a *situation*. The danger that the military assigned specialists to. That was how seriously they were taking all of this. And it made it hard for me to keep from doing the same.

Axel's brows quirked down, and he shook his head. "Sorry. With people like you who need protection. The agency is no more, gutted by infighting and politics. A lot of agencies like that had their funding pulled when the military started hiring contractors. Tucker and I kept working together and started an executive security protection company together. We make an excellent team and enjoy the work. The guy we're leaving here is someone we've worked with before. He's former military too, a sniper. Which means he knows everything about countersniping. We will leave your ranch in expert hands."

"Are you a wolf-shifter too?" I knew he was a shifter, but not what kind. I didn't know if wolves ever worked closely with other shifters, but they were apparently friends with at least some local bear-shifters, and I was too aware of how spotty my knowledge was as an outsider.

Axel turned to me, but without the surprised look I still half expected. "I am. Born and bred. We were told that you're familiar with shifters. But you're not one yourself." Not a question, but a statement.

"It's kind of a long story. But since finding out about shifters, I've noticed some things after a few years out here. There seem to be quite a few shifters in the area. Maybe it's because we're so isolated out here."

Axel shrugged. "I'm originally from New York, and Tucker's from Chicago. We're based out here now, in Billings. Our kind is everywhere. Just depends where our people gravitated. A lot of us prefer rural areas, and that's most of Montana."

"It's hard to think of shifters, especially wolves, in a big city. Wolves and bears living in this area makes sense to me. Not so much in the middle of a giant city with its smells and lack of privacy. I mean, Billings is big enough, but New York?"

Axel laughed, a rich, deep sound. "You realize that shifters can drive out to the country when they want to run wild, right? And that many of us spend most of our time in human form?"

I scowled. "You're making fun of me, aren't you?" I was still feeling a little hypersensitive, though I had calmed down a lot around them.

He was still smiling at me, but it wasn't a mocking smile. "No, not really. Well...maybe just a little. I like to challenge people's perceptions of me." The smile faded, and his face took on a much kinder expression. "That really wasn't fair of me. You're under a great deal of stress. I shouldn't have said what I did."

"What did you say now, Axel?" Tucker strode across the yard toward us. "Never mind. I'm sure it was something inappropriate."

I eyed Tucker. *Oh, like you're one to talk, buddy.*

"What do you want to do with the vehicles?" Axel ignored the jab, and I thought maybe this was how they dealt with the stress that must come with this kind of work.

"Benny is going to rotate them in and out of the garage, keep some in the driveway. Clarify that there's someone here."

Tucker looked up at the sky. "We need to get going. Looks like snow. Smells like it, too."

He was right. In the span of time since we'd gotten the horses ready, the temperature had dropped, the sky had taken on the color of pewter, and the wind had shifted, now carrying the scent of snow.

"Got everything you need?" Tucker took Storm's reins from me.

"I'm all set. I'm a little worried about you guys, though. Try not to let my horses dump you off." I held back a smile. Maybe I could get a jab in once in a while and insert a little levity into the situation.

Both men turned to look at me, Axel with an arched eyebrow and cocky grin, Tucker with a faint scowl, both ready with a retort. I held up my hands.

"I know, I know. You're *always* ready." Before they could answer back, I swung up on Mary. "Let's hit the trail, men."

I still wondered what living with these men would be like. Not because they were shifters, but because they were so damned proud that they could dish out teasing all day long but, apparently, couldn't take it. Well, they would have to learn. Because I was nobody's doormat, and every time these shifters pushed me, I would be right there, pushing back.

$$\maltese \quad 6 \quad \maltese$$

It made me nervous to cross the open pasture now that I knew someone with a rifle could hide in the surrounding woods. Tucker rode in front of me, Axel behind. Both of them on watch. But for the quarter-mile between the ranch and the trees, I felt exposed. The wind had picked up, chilling me and playing tricks with sounds. I wanted to kick Mary into a gallop and get out of the open. Instead, I kept still, avoided fidgeting, breathed deep, and tried to keep calm, knowing any anxiety I showed would scare horses already made jumpy by the fire and its aftermath.

All three horses already snorted and danced a little when the shifting wind brought the smell of burned timber to us. They didn't like being reminded of the fire any more than I did.

When we entered the cover of the evergreens, I let out the breath I'd been holding for the last several yards. It was like entering a new world, a dark green space where the wind died away, the only sounds the crunch of the horses' hooves through the thin crust of snow and their soft snorts. There was still the possibility of a sniper in the woods, but they would have trouble getting close enough for a clear shot now without us noticing them.

I trotted up beside Tucker. "There's a trailhead about a mile from here, at the base of the mountain. It's the only trail that goes up. If anyone's been through here, you should be able to see their tracks."

Tucker nodded. "Good to know."

He didn't seem interested in continuing the conversation, and I dropped back to my place in the middle of our little group. I felt alone among strangers, who might have been professional and experienced with this work, but were still strangers. That they could turn into giant wolves wasn't as comforting as it could have been.

The ride up the mountain stayed quiet like that, the horses and the wind in the branches providing the only consistent noise. The two men were on watch, glancing around at everything as we rode. When I looked at each of them, they met my gaze but spoke little.

An hour into our ride, flakes filtered down through the pine boughs, tossed by the wind into random patterns. The temperature dropped further. I could see my breath puffing white ahead of me. The horses snorted little clouds.

Damn, here we go. I hope we don't end up in an actual blizzard up here.

When we came out of the deep pine forest, the wind hit us hard, snow flying madly through the air. Tucker stopped scanning the ground, but I knew the swirling wind and extra inches of snow would have obscured any tracks quickly. I pulled up the hood on my jacket and shivered. It was going to be a miserable ride up the rest of the mountain. But this had been my idea, and there was no turning back now.

The trail was steep, twisting around and then up the backside of the mountain, temporarily hiding my land from sight. The snow was falling harder now, in thick white curtains that contracted the world down to a snowy circle around us. *No wonder they were so impatient to get going. I should have listened.*

Tucker kept following the obscured trail, and despite whatever thoughts I'd had about him, he knew how to navigate through this tough country. I glanced back at Axel. He rode easily, confidently, letting Jane choose her path, but clearly in control of the animal.

Okay, good. At least I don't have to worry about Jane getting jumpy because he won't ease up on the reins and tossing him off the edge of the trail. Storm seemed calm too. *I thought shifters would make horses skittish, like normal predators do. I guess I really don't know that much about them.*

I just hoped the man they'd left behind at the ranch did right by Henry, my animals, and my land.

The weather continued to deteriorate quickly, the snow thickening, the wind howling around us. Tucker was a darker shadow among gray shapes of rocks and stunted trees.

The surrounding whiteness disoriented me. I couldn't see Tucker's tracks in the snow. *Had he gotten off the trail, or had I?* For a horrible moment, I panicked, pulling hard on Mary's reins, bringing her to an abrupt stop. *Okay. Calm down. Get your bearings.*

"Alina!" Axel maneuvered Jane beside me on the trail. "What's wrong?"

I almost lost his voice in the wind. I shook my head, pointing ahead into the swirling storm.

"I'm not sure where we are." The wind pulled the words out of my mouth. "I think we're lost."

Jane pranced beside me, Axel holding her tossing head. "Where's Tucker?" he asked.

"I don't know. I can't even see him in this whiteout. That's kind of the problem, and I'd rather stop than get more lost."

"I get it. Give him a minute. He'll notice we've fallen behind." I could barely feel his gloved hand on my arm, but it steadied me a little all the same.

"Okay," I mumbled and did my best to wait while the cold soaked deeper into my bones.

Suddenly, Axel pointed. "There. He's ahead of you."

I looked up, watching as Storm's black form emerged from

the snow. Tucker guided the horse back down the trail toward us until we formed a tight group. "Everything all right?" Tucker questioned.

"Just nearly blind in this whiteout. You rode too far ahead for us to see you." No accusation in my voice.

He nodded, not apologizing but at least not saying anything snide in response. "I caught sight of your property. Cabin, small stables? Old well out front?"

I nodded, huffing with relief. "That's the one." Finally, a stroke of luck. Or maybe it had been his keen wolf's senses.

"It's just over this ridge. Come on." He turned Storm, and I kicked Mary forward so she followed the big black horse. I rode with my head down, trusting Storm and Mary, and trying to trust Tucker. Just as long as he remembered not to go dashing ahead into a whiteout again.

Mary finally lurched to a stop, and I looked up. We were in the clearing at the top of the slope, the cabin a dim shape on the other side. I'd never been so happy to see that little building in my life. I urged Mary forward, heading for the modest stables attached to the cabin. I wanted to get the horses unsaddled, tended, and safe in their shelter before anything else. I was glad as hell that we kept it stocked with hay, bedding bales, and bins of feed. Otherwise, we would have had to haul all that up in this mess.

By the time we reached the stable, Tucker had dismounted, holding Storm's reins, and was pulling open the door.

Axel dismounted, holding Mary's bridle while I slid out of the saddle. We led the horses into the stable. They'd built it right up against the cottage, sharing a stone wall with it that showed the outline of the hearth and chimney built into its other side. It was cold inside with no fire going in the main cottage, but it was still a blessed relief to be out of the wind. I stood in the doorway to give the men room to pull off the saddles, looking out at the snow-filled clearing. It was almost impossible to tell the difference between the edge of the world and the edge of the sky.

"Here, we've got the tack off two of them. Let's get them bedded down."

I turned toward Axel, nodding. The three roomy box stalls were bare-floored right now to keep from attracting mice. I pushed past them into the storage area beyond and started pulling out bales of bedding straw. "Toss two of these into each," I said over my shoulder as I reached for another.

Tucker dropped Storm's saddle on the rack, moving to Mary and pulling off hers. Axel was finishing up getting Jane settled in her stall. I got the last of the bales out and stepped into the nearest stall to cut and spread. My arms ached with exhaustion, but I kept going, not wanting to show weakness in front of these men.

With the horses taken care of, we walked outside, shoved the door closed against the wind, then struggled around to the front of the cabin. Snow had drifted against the door, and I brushed it away with my foot. The key was on my key ring, and for a panicked moment, I patted my pockets. I couldn't remember grabbing them, but I was never without them. Finally, I found them in my front jeans pocket and pulled them out with shaking hands. *Shit, what is wrong with my head right now?*

But I knew. I hadn't slept properly in four days now, I had fought the wind the entire way up there, and unlike them, I didn't have shifter stamina.

Axel took the keys from me, holding up the only skeleton key. I nodded, and he fitted it into the lock. The door swung open, a flutter of snow spilling across the floor. It was almost completely black inside, the storm shutters and thermal curtains letting precious little light through.

We got inside, Tucker slamming the door behind us, dropping my pack and his by the door. I saw green spots everywhere from being out in the whiteout as my eyes adjusted.

"Give me a second." I reached for the oil lantern that hung

by the door, managing all on my own to strike a match and light it. The glow it cast pushed the shadows into the corners but didn't dispel them completely. For that, we would need to get the generator going. And that would mean going back out in this mess, something I would not be up to for a while.

Tucker shook the snow off his jacket, shrugging out of it, then hanging it on one hook by the door. Axel was already in the kitchen area of the cabin, really just part of the living room, but with cabinets and a wood-burning cookstove. He was opening cabinet doors, looking in drawers, and nodding as he poked around. As I rubbed warmth back into my hands, he returned to where I stood, apparently satisfied with what he had found.

"You have a survivalist mentality, Miss Glory. It will serve you well in this situation."

"Yes, well, you never quite know when you must get away for a few weeks." Like whenever Dad and his entourage deigned to grace me with his presence unexpectedly. It had only happened twice, but showing up to my empty house and being forced to call me and try to convince me to come back had deterred him from any more surprise visits.

Tucker looked up from the hearth, where he was patiently feeding small logs onto the fire. He'd taken kindling from the wood box in the corner and a handful of pinecones from the woven basket next to it, and he was doing a credible job of getting the fire going.

"That's mostly Henry's doing. He chose all that stuff that we brought up here, all the prepackaged meals. You know, just add water."

Tucker laughed. "We're pretty familiar with MREs. I can't tell you how many of those I've eaten. Same for Axel. They're better than ration bars, at least."

I sat down on the couch as Axel grabbed his bag. The first tentative waves of heat reached me, and I held my hands toward the fire. My fingers were sore from the cold. They got worse, the tips going red, before finally starting to tingle as the pain faded. But I was in one piece, no signs of frostbite. We had made it.

I wondered how Tucker managed without a jacket. Maybe it was a wolf-shifter thing. Axel still wore his, and I pulled mine more tightly around me. It was below freezing outside, not much warmer in here, and I knew it would take some time for the cabin to warm up.

"You seem pretty experienced in the wild for a couple of city boys." The joke came out flat thanks to my tired tone, and Tucker snorted. I pulled the thick, knitted afghan off the back of the couch, tucking it around my legs.

The gigantic fireplace was set into the stone wall the cabin shared with the small stable, and the heated stone would warm it up. It was an old-fashioned system I had been forced to supplement with propane heaters in the past, but this was December, not deep winter. Hopefully, the storm would blow over soon, and the weather would finally rise above freezing.

"Here. Come sit down here, closer to the fire." Axel tugged at the afghan, pulling it off my legs. I slipped off the couch onto the floor, resting my back against the couch, stretching my legs toward the fire. It might not have been warmer, but it was cozier. Tucker added another log to the fire and then sat back beside me. Axel came around the other side of the couch, dropping gracefully on my other side.

"I think I have something that'll warm us up." He reached into his bag and pulled out a bottle, holding it out to me. I took it and glanced at the label. *Jesus, they brought fucking Glenlivet—a single malt scotch—as travel whiskey.*

"You know your whiskey," I commented. "I'll get some glasses." I went to get up, but Tucker put a hand on my arm.

"I think we can do without glasses." He took the bottle from me and opened it. "Ladies first."

I took the bottle back, taking a long pull. The whiskey was cold, but it still bit my tongue. Going down, it felt like liquid fire, and a heartbeat later, it hit my stomach, causing a mini explosion of heat. I closed my eyes, leaning back against the couch. "Phew. That was good."

"You looked like you needed that." Tucker's voice was close to my ear, and I opened my eyes, turning to look at him. He reached over and took the bottle, putting it to his lips, eyes never leaving mine as he took a swallow. He lowered the bottle, his face only inches from mine. Then he broke into a wry little grin. "I think I needed that, too."

The warmth inside me spread outward, and it wasn't all because of the alcohol. Tucker held my gaze as I reached out, taking back the bottle. Our fingers brushed, and a brief shiver of excitement ran through me.

"Thanks." I lifted the bottle, a little sloppy, a drop or two spilling. I ran my tongue out, savoring the burn on my lips.

"My turn." Fingers touched mine, and I turned to find Axel leaning in, reaching for the bottle. The tingle Tucker had started intensified. I held the bottle, not wanting to break contact. Axel eased the bottle out of my hand, slowly taking a long pull.

The fire crackled, throwing heat over my legs and into my face. The room was still a little chilly, with that odd combination of temperatures you got with a roaring fire as your only heat source. That and sitting between two healthy specimens of manhood. Between the fire, the whiskey, and Axel and Tucker, I was finally warm enough to shed my jacket. I sat forward, shrugging out of it. Tucker tugged it the rest of the way off, tossing it onto the couch.

"Does this place have a name?" Axel asked.

The bottle crossed in front of me, heading back in Tucker's direction. I finished pulling off my boots, then turned to Axel to answer.

"Echo Lake. How did you know it had a name?"

"Most places do." He shrugged. "At least, the places that mean something to their owners have names. Where's the lake?"

For the first time in what seemed like an eternity, I let myself relax. Talking about anything besides the fire and the sniper was a welcome relief. I knew most of how I felt was because of the alcohol, but I didn't care. The knots in my shoulders untied themselves, and I let out a long sigh.

"Wisconsin. My grandparents' cottage was on Echo Lake. I used to go there every summer. This place reminded me of that, so I named it in its honor."

I closed my eyes, remembering those summers. It was back when dear old Dad had been between wives, after my mother had gotten so sick of him, she had taken off on both of us. He had become even more insufferable with me during those years, reminded of his runaway wife as I grew to look more like her every year. But his parents, well...they were nothing like him, and that meant I had gotten a blessed break from him out in the countryside all summer long.

"So, you have some family that you're close with," Tucker remarked. "I heard your father's a giant pain in the ass."

"Had. They both died a few years back. And yes, he really is." But I didn't want to go into a rant about my controlling, sexist, overly nosy dad, or my mood would start dropping again. Instead, I hunted around in my dull, tired mind for a better topic.

I took the bottle back from Tucker, taking another drink. "Did you know there's a ghost story that goes along with this cabin?"

Axel made an impatient hand-me-the-bottle sound, and I let him take it. Tucker stretched out on the floor next to me, resting his head on his hand. "Can't say that I do. What is it?"

"The cabin originally belonged to a miner named Ezra Johnson. He staked a claim, along with two friends. This was in the 1850s, during the Gold Rush. Not long after, strange things started happening. Miners with neighboring claims started turning up dead. There were reports of a giant rogue bear being sighted in the area. But nothing seemed to bother the three miners here. They kept mining, kept finding more gold. They started getting pretty successful and began expanding. They bought up the claims of the dead miners around them. Hunting parties went out, but no one could find evidence of any bear, rogue or otherwise. But they found footprints, large human footprints. Word got around that Ezra had someone working for him, someone big and scary who was killing off the competition."

The bottle was back in front of me, and I took another swallow, passing it to Tucker. I felt better. My feet were still a little sore, but they had color in the toes, and my legs were warm.

"There were rumors in New Fane of magic, of witchcraft, of something evil lurking up here in the wilderness. People whispered about a giant man living in the shed out back, doing Ezra's bidding. Killing for Ezra and his friends."

"Wait, is this a ghost story or a serial-killer story?" Tucker sounded a little confused. Maybe even concerned, and I knew why.

"Most people think it's a ghost story, because they don't know what else to call it. Me, I've got my suspicions. But no proof, of course. Just the stories." Of course, my suspicion was that Ezra, or an unnamed friend who lived with the three, had been a bear-shifter. Because as I had already learned from Shamus, not all shifters were decent people.

Tucker nodded slowly and took his turn pulling from the bottle. "All right. Go on."

"Well, as often happens in these situations, friends don't always stay friends when there's money involved. Ezra turned up in town, claiming that 'the bear' had killed his two friends. He bought out their shares and cashed in what some say was over a million dollars in gold. Ezra disappeared shortly after that. The killings stopped."

I considered my company for a moment, wondering if I should bring up my theory. Maybe it wasn't a ghost story. Maybe it was a bear story. A greedy, asshole, shape-shifting bear story. But would they take it well if I laid the complete mess at the feet of one of their kind?

"And what do you think happened?" Axel had stretched out on the rug, head resting on one of the couch cushions. His chiseled features contrasted with Tucker's rough-around-the-edges looks. Even their clothing played up their differences. Tucker wore a plaid flannel shirt, one or two buttons undone. Axel had on a black turtleneck that fit him perfectly, outlining broad shoulders and muscled arms. For a minute, I cast a few surreptitious glances between the men, wondering not for the first time how I'd ended up here with them.

For a moment, the booze loosened my self-control enough that I started thinking about the possibilities of having two desirable men alone with me up in this very private cabin. *There are other things we could do to warm us up,* I caught myself thinking.

Then I shook myself. *Calm down, girl. You barely know them, and Tucker's been a jerk. Take it slowly, and don't let the Glenlivet do the talking.*

"I don't have a horse in that race," I replied. "I think it's a wonderful story to tell around the fire." I thought back to the first time I'd heard the story, sitting around outside in the dark, with my older cousins scaring the crap out of me as we had shared around a much cheaper bottle of booze. I was glad I got along with my dad's family better than with him, but the bunch of them really loved their alcohol, and the cousins loved freaking me out too. "I could toss out some theories, but that's all they would be."

"You think it was a shifter?" Axel lifted an eyebrow in my direction.

"Maybe. Even after I found out about you guys, I never wanted to speculate too much. Maybe the guy was a bear-shifter. Maybe he was just a murdering jackass good at hiding bodies. Or maybe there really was some kind of ghost or something else involved. No way of knowing now." I was being more diplomatic than usual, but that was a lot easier to do now that I was warm and out of danger.

Axel nodded. "Fair enough."

"How do you know so much about us anyway?" Tucker had gotten up and was stoking a fire in the cookstove. "You seem pretty calm about knowing, and obviously, you don't run around telling people."

"Of course not. You've heard of my dad. Very few people I've ever met are bigger gossips. In fact, I don't trust him not to leverage your existence to further his career in some fucked-up way." Dad was very progressive on some issues, but he was still a goddamned Washington politician, greedy for any advantage, especially in the polls.

Tucker grunted in disgust and nodded as he filled up the kettle. "Yeah. It's pretty damn clear you must take after your mom, because that guy's a piece of work."

"You said it." I never tried to deny who my dad was under the surface, or fight against criticism of him. "But yeah, I don't talk about shifters except with shifters. I'm really careful not to bring it up with anyone else, not even people close to me."

"Why not?" Axel gazed into my eyes like he was trying to read my thoughts.

"First off, I don't feel like making any enemies. And second, if news broke wide about your existence, I don't want to think about what would happen. Everything from would-be monster hunters riding around in their pickups with guns, to government guys trying to put you in a fucking lab, I suspect." I rubbed the end of my nose, which was still prickling from the cold. At least the booze was easing my discomfort while I warmed up.

The two exchanged surprised glances. "You're probably right," Axel said after a moment. "I don't imagine most normal people take that into consideration, but yes, it would be a disaster for all shifters. But that still doesn't explain how you learned enough to come to this decision."

"Shamus McKenzie." I smirked slightly. "He's a wolf-shifter."

"A wolf-shifter?" Tucker lifted an eyebrow as he turned back from putting the kettle on. "Oh, where's your coffee?"

"Blue ceramic jar next to the hand grinder. And yeah, Shamus is a wolf-shifter. He lives in town above the Blue Moon bar. Part-time bouncer, full-time drunk, but I guess they put up with him because he's family." I rubbed my hands together and stretched them toward the fire.

"So, what happened?" Axel sniffed appreciatively as the smell of freshly ground beans hit the air. Tucker must have loved his coffee, because he was grinding up a batch.

"Bored one night, with things under control at the ranch, I picked the Blue Moon as my new local bar to have a few beers at. Didn't know if I would come across anyone worth meeting, but I figured I'd give it a shot. And the Blue Moon isn't bad as bars go. If Shamus weren't around there, I would probably go back." I watched Tucker work in the flickering glow from the lantern and the fire, the gold-orange light playing over his tall form enticingly.

I carried on. "So, I came walking into the bar, and the first thing I noticed was everyone looking at me. Not really a surprise since it doesn't look like a place that attracts outsiders, but it was still a little weird. I sat down, got a beer and chili fries, and people eventually got back to their conversations. All except for this one guy." I shuddered slightly. Shamus had been that mix of sleazy and slightly menacing that reminded me way too much of my dad once he had a few drinks in him...times about three. Worse, Shamus had been just as hot in his own way as Axel and Tucker, though he had ruined it by being a drunken mess with a shitty attitude. "He started looking at me like a prime rib he was getting ready to cut into, and I knew he was about to come over and say something disgusting. And, of course, he did."

I sighed and closed my eyes, remembering the scene, the smell of stale beer, whiskey, and musk coming off the unwashed idiot who had stomped up to my table like he expected to haul me over his shoulder and walk off with me like some cave dweller. "And the first thing he said to me was that we were going to be fucking by the end of the night, and that if I knew what was good for me, I wouldn't make him work hard for my pussy."

Tucker made a disgusted noise, and Axel winced. Hopefully now, they were getting an inkling of why I didn't enjoy having orders barked at me by random, overconfident men. Or any men. Dad had burned through nearly all of my patience for that, and Shamus had demolished the rest.

I went on, while in the back of my head, I wondered whether overbearing idiots like him were common among wolf-shifters, or whether Shamus was their equivalent of an omega wolf and had been desperately overcompensating. "I just looked at him, because whiskey confidence makes idiots out of a lot of men, and this one was clearly an asshole to begin with. Then I told him to go the hell back to his seat and rethink his approach."

I paused before continuing, "Now, I've dealt with men who thought they could bully a woman into bed. And because of a lifetime of experience with my dad, I'm a veteran at dealing with a man who loves to bark orders at me." I spared another look at Tucker, who glanced back, having the grace to look just slightly embarrassed.

"I'm guessing Shamus didn't back down at all," Tucker stated.

"Nope. He just stood there and kept pushing, adding the typical sexual insults you usually see when you reject a guy online. But, you know, right there to my face."

Axel snorted. "How classy." Sarcasm dripped from his tone.

I shrugged. "Finally, I gave up and told him to fuck off. Some guys at the bar snickered, and so did the bartender. I figured they'd seen that dick strike out before, and I didn't really think anything of it when he growled at me and then sulked off back to his table."

"Uh oh," Tucker muttered. "Mugs?"

"Second cupboard from the left." I flexed my hands, which were finally starting to feel warm. "After he backed off, I spent a good hour downing two beers, finishing my chili fries, and talking to a few people. But the whole goddamned time, the asshole was glaring at me like he wanted to murder me."

"He's a jackass," Axel snapped.

"For sure," Tucker chimed in.

"Anyway, I guess his ego got bruised. Or maybe he was looking for an excuse to beat on a woman. Because when I finally got up, the bastard followed me out."

Axel's brows drew together. "Nobody did anything?"

"No, they just watched, or so I thought. Turns out, the rest of his...pack?" Axel nodded, and I went on. "Was used to this behavior, and so when he followed me out, I didn't notice a few of his pack members slipping out the back, quietly circling around to the parking lot."

"Not sure if that's a good thing or a bad thing," Tucker admitted as he dug my coffee cone and filters out of one drawer.

"Turned out to be a good thing, but I'm getting to that." I stared impatiently at the kettle, wishing it would come to a boil already. The whiskey offered comfort but not actual warmth, and it was making me sleepy, when I needed some energy. "He calls me out, yelling, tossing insults, telling me I had better turn around and 'come make this up' to him. I guess I should have been more scared, but all his bullshit did was piss me off. I pulled out my belt knife, turned around, and told him he needed to get his drunk ass back inside before I stabbed him in the dick. He just looked at me in shock. Guys like that never expect push-back. I'm not sure he even knew what to do with me, but the booze in his system apparently had some ideas." I paused. "He started backing off, and I turned around and headed for my car. But then I heard a terrible sound behind me. Turns out it was him unzipping his goddamn pants."

I shook my head. "I gripped my knife and looked back, expecting him to have his dick out. Instead, it was him as a wolf in the middle of the parking lot."

They both stared at me, now completely horrified. "Jesus Christ," Tucker muttered. "Glad it was late at night in a small town. A stunt like that in the age of smartphones could have exposed us all."

"I know. Or at least, I've figured that out now. I didn't know shit back then. But this guy didn't care who saw him, he was that drunk and stupid—and that pissed off. And so, instead of a naked drunk coming after me, I was suddenly facing a huge, snarling wolf."

"Did he hurt you?" Axel frowned, sitting up straighter, watching me intently.

"He never even got close to me, but he sure tried. I ended up on the roof of my car, taking swipes at him with my knife when he tried to jump up, yelling the entire time because I didn't know what the hell was going on. I don't even know how I got up there before he got to me."

"Sounds like pure adrenaline." Axel smoothed back his hair with a hand. "Lucky thing. So, what happened? Did someone intervene? You said some of his pack members snuck out the back."

"Yes, that's exactly what happened. This big dark-gray wolf, maybe twice Shamus's mass, came barreling around the corner of the building and slammed into him. Knocked him completely off his feet. And they fought. It went so fast that all I saw was a big, hairy blur and heard lots of snarling. Shamus got pinned and then grabbed by the scruff and hauled back to his feet. Finally, the bigger wolf herded him over to his clothes, bullied him into grabbing his pants in his teeth, and back around the corner they went. And I was just left there, standing on top of my car, watching them and wondering what the hell just happened."

They were both staring at me now. The teakettle had finally started sputtering a little, though the whistle hadn't sounded yet.

"So, I'm just climbing down when one guy from the bar comes back around the corner and asks me if I'm all right. I don't even know what to tell him. I just say, 'I'm not hurt, but I am kind of questioning my sanity.' I was shocked as hell when he laughed. The guy's name was Jericho. I don't know what position he held in the pack, but it must have been pretty important because he came out representing all of them. When he was sure I was all right and would not go running off, screaming about wolves, he offered me another drink and an explanation. And I agreed, because I didn't know what the hell else to do."

More nodding. They couldn't take their eyes off me now. "So, the Blue Moon is the local pack hangout, then?" Axel looked like he was making a mental note.

"Yeah, I guess so. They didn't offer a lot of specifics while I was there. But this guy Jericho, he sat me down, gave me some facts of life about shifters, and promised me Shamus would never bother me again if, of course, I didn't talk about my encounter with anyone. I agreed to the deal, but after that, I started noticing things. How many of you there are around the local area. How you look, smell, and act different from humans. I don't even do it that consciously. But I just started noticing glaring differences. I guess something in my head is a little wary of a shifter getting the drop on me again. But that doesn't mean I hate shifters. Not even when the first one I met was an absolute asshole."

The teakettle finally whistled, and Tucker took it off the stovetop to pour steaming water through the mound of coffee grounds in the filter. "I'm glad that you don't hold that asshole's behavior against an entire race," he commented with surprising sincerity.

"Most humans whose first experience with a shifter is negative let that shape their entire view of all shifters," Axel elaborated as he stretched out beside me. He squinted happily as he scooted closer to the fire, reminding me of a dog ready to roll over on his back with his paws up and start wiggling. It was so cute that it distracted me from the serious subject.

"Yeah, well, I've never been a torches-and-pitchforks kind of woman. Besides, I would not let some drunk, predatory asshole determine what I thought about an entire race."

"Did you ever think this Shamus guy could be responsible for the fire?" Tucker deftly transferred the coffee cone to the next mug, added a scoop of fresh grounds and poured the water. The rich smell of the coffee was unbearably tempting.

"Not really. I mean, he was a violent drunk not a schemer, and his go-to is wolfing out and chasing people. If something had ripped up my sheep or horses, I would have suspected him. But the fire? That sniper? No. Didn't even cross my mind." I blinked in surprise as Tucker brought me the first cup of coffee. "Thank you."

"Don't mention it." He went back to the counter, a brief smile on his face. "Especially if I can get you to cook up one of those roasts I saw in the chest freezer."

I gave him one of the first genuine smiles I had managed since the fire. "Deal."

❧ 7 ❧

The cabin's on fire. The doors are nailed shut. They will shoot us if we crawl out of the windows.

We're all going to burn.

I gasped awake, covered in cold sweat, and for several moments, I did not understand where I was. Dull red light flickered over dark-paneled walls and exposed beams. Beyond the blackout curtains on the windows, I could hear a snowstorm scouring the glass.

The cabin.

Everything came flooding back to me. The fire, the craziness of the last four days, the two wolf-shifters, the harrowing ride up here. Slowly, I got my bearings.

I was on one of the two folding beds with a memory foam mattress that normally sat in a closet off the bathroom. I could hear soft snoring from the other one and from the couch. I must not have slept long. I was still full from a roast beef dinner and dizzy from the scotch. It was getting cold. I forced myself up to feed the fire some more logs. It grew quickly, splashing brighter orange light around the cabin's interior. I heard one of them stir and looked back at Tucker on the couch, frowning slightly in his sleep as the firelight strengthened. I quietly added another log and then went back to my bed to bundle myself in my blanket.

I sat up, wrapping my arms around my knees under the afghan, staring into the fire. I was still a little more than halfway drunk, and my mind still raced with chaotic thoughts about the fire, about leaving Henry at the ranch, about why someone would want me dead when I was publicly estranged from the father they had a problem with. And, of course, why in the middle of all this chaos, I found myself hopelessly attracted to not one, but both of my new bodyguards.

I couldn't even choose between them. The attraction to both was too strong. Tucker's blond ruggedness contrasted nicely with Axel's dark, polished good looks.

Tucker challenged me, and sometimes annoyed me, but seemed drawn by the push-pull between us, even impressed when I stood up to him.

Axel was friendlier and more easygoing. I had thought at first that he was more secure than Tucker, but now I realized that Tucker was that used to having his authority recognized. *Was it a rich guy thing, or was he the leader of his pack?* It was hard to tell. Axel didn't defer to him. In fact, the two constantly seemed to banter and take shots at each other as easily as a couple of brothers.

I frowned. Figuring out the dynamic between them was just as difficult as figuring out which one I wanted more.

It's not like I have to choose anyway.

There's no way they're both interested in me. They probably have women throwing themselves at them all the time. And I really didn't want to make an idiot out of myself.

Stuck in this place, hiding from a sniper and arsonist, I was keenly aware of my own loneliness. I hadn't touched a man since breaking off my engagement and leaving Washington. I had thought about dating, gone to a few bars and coffee shops to see what the prospects were, and laughed my way through a ridiculous night on a "good" dating site where men slinging dick pics at women too young for them had seemed to be the common practice. But nothing had ever come of my dating attempts.

I rarely got depressed over my lack of romantic prospects. But here it was, a week from Christmas, and it was the only time of year when the lack of love and sex in my life really hit me hard. I didn't know if it was a seasonal disorder or just from having spent half a decade "celebrating" Christmas alone. Maybe I felt the aloneness more keenly this year because the possibility of spending the holiday with two strangers who didn't exactly strike me as the Christmas type was real. And being with two hot guys who probably didn't have any romantic interest in me was just rubbing me emotionally raw.

I took a deep, shuddering breath. Finally, I forced myself to lie back down. My eyes brimmed over, and cold tears spilled down my cheeks. I held still, ordering myself not to sob as I trembled under the blanket. *This would pass.* I was just overtired and dealing with a lot of stress.

"You okay?"

I looked over, startled, and saw that Tucker's eyes were open, and he was watching me from the couch. His brow furrowed with concern.

I nodded, though I wasn't feeling okay at all. "Just a nightmare," I murmured. "Guess that shouldn't be a surprise."

He sighed, looking a little grim. "After what you've been through? No. Not a surprise at all." He got up to poke at the fire and add a handful of kindling to my haphazard stack of logs. "But you need to try for more sleep. It's damn clear you're deprived."

"Yes," I mumbled. "I guess you see this kind of thing a lot."

He nodded. "Most of our clients are afraid of what might happen to them if the people after them win. But don't worry. We haven't failed a client yet."

I stared at him desolately as he sat back down on the couch, then flopped over lazily. "That's good to know."

He smirked. "You don't sound very convinced."

"It's not that. I've got no doubts you're competent. This whole situation is just messing with me." And lying there in the dark, talking with him, made the loneliness gnaw at me that much harder. I remembered his comforting hug and craved another. Craved more than that, but I had absolutely no idea how to ask. So instead, I lay back down and closed my eyes, trying to relax enough that I could sleep again.

It must have worked, because I woke up to sunlight trickling through the gaps in the curtains and the faint call of crows.

It was morning, and the storm was over. Fresh logs crackled in both wood stoves, and when I looked over, I saw both men perched at my kitchen table, drinking coffee and chatting softly.

"No signs that anyone followed us up," Tucker was saying. "The trail's snowed in anyway. We should be safe up here unless we run out of supplies."

"Good. Maybe this was a better idea than Billings. Out there, a hitter could hide in a crowd. They could only get at us here if they had a fucking gunship. And even then, we would hear them coming."

Something about that didn't sound right to me. Whoever had shot at me had done so from the woods, unseen, unheard. The dogs had barked, but as Henry had said, they barked at everything. "What if whoever it is knows their way around the woods?" I asked.

Axel laughed. "I doubt they're as good as one wolf, let alone two."

I nodded, but I couldn't keep the little frown off my face.

Tucker tilted his head. "What is it, Alina?"

"Just a nagging worry. Probably nerves. Never mind." I didn't want to insult them by sounding like I doubted their expertise.

"No, seriously, what is it?" Axel brought me coffee and sat beside me as I sat up and sipped it.

"I just... Whoever shot through my window would have had to climb a tall tree to even get the right angle to shoot me in my bed. They got in and out with no one seeing them. They knew what they were doing. This wasn't just some newbie with his deer-hunting rifle."

Tucker frowned and came over, sitting on my other side. "You have a point."

"Any word from your guy back at the farm?"

"Benny? We talked to him this morning. He's bored to death. All quiet." Tucker's gaze searched my face. "Are you worried you won't get back in time for Christmas or something?"

I scoffed slightly. "I barely celebrate Christmas. Have done little besides dinner and a gift exchange for years."

Tucker frowned. "Why not?"

I let out a laugh. "My father. He has this way of wrecking things like holidays by using them as a chance for self-promotion."

"What do you mean?" The concern on Axel's face surprised me. "How did he ruin the holidays for you?"

"It's been a lot of things over the years." I pursed my lips, thinking back. "Trying to match me with creepy friends his age is big. So was the way some of his big donors would sexually harass my mother back before she left. Definitely one thing that drove her away. Christmas was just another round of that, but with a decorated tree and thirsty old guys leering at me as they parked themselves under the mistletoe."

Tucker shuddered. "That's fucked up. That would put me off Christmas and the holidays too. Sucks, though. The holiday season really can be a lot of fun."

I smiled sadly. "You sound like Elizabeth. She's the one responsible for all the holiday decorations at my place. If she could, she'd probably come trekking up the mountain with a Christmas turkey and lots of sides just to make sure I got my plate."

Axel smiled. "She sounds like good people."

"The best, her and Henry. I don't know what I would do without them. I just hope Henry's safe down there." If anything happened to him, I'd never forgive myself.

"Well, look," Tucker said, with that self-assurance I used to find a lot more irritating. Somehow, it had become a comfort in the last twelve hours, maybe because I could draw on it when I had nothing. "Once we deal with this mess, we'll show you what a real Christmas party is like. That sound good?"

I couldn't help but smile. I knew he was distracting me from the scary possibility of a sniper in the woods, and of my friend, animals, and ranch being in danger. But that distraction was very welcome.

"You know what? Maybe I'll take you up on that."

$$\text{8}$$

The three of us fell into a routine after a few days at the cabin. The snowstorm had left a thick blanket on the ground, and every morning I woke to discover the same two sets of paw prints marking it from my new bodyguards' early morning patrols.

Axel, an early riser, made the coffee. We worked together making breakfast. After that, I called Henry to see what was going on. He had nothing to report. The lambs were doing well, as were their mothers. The dogs started barking now and again, but when he let them loose, they just ended up chasing squirrels around. His family missed him when he spent nights in the sheep barn, and he tried to make up for it by taking meals with them and spending the end of his day making snowmen and pulling sleds for his children.

Elizabeth, nervous about the fire and the would-be sniper, had listened when I had told her not to visit until it was all over. She called twice. Me once and Henry once, making sure we were all right. It worried her that the Christmas dinner we had planned would have to wait until New Year's because of this mess. I forced myself not to admit that it didn't really matter to me. Even my yearly feast with Elizabeth, her sons, Henry, and his family couldn't break my Christmas depression. I knew she meant well, and I didn't want to ruin it for her.

There was no sign of anyone unwanted walking the grounds. The snow would have shown it, and the only human footprints Henry saw around besides his and his family's were Benny's. He could tell them easily, because they were even bigger and deeper than his own.

Benny himself was distant but capable, walking the grounds but offering little in the way of conversation. Henry didn't like him but couldn't fault his competence. He couldn't even say why he didn't like him. "Just my gut," he explained one morning, and I wondered if it was the wolf in Benny that bothered him. Weirdly, though, Henry hadn't seemed to have any problem with Tucker or Axel. Maybe Benny was just more abrasive. But the comment still stuck in my mind... Henry had good instincts.

I wanted to bring up the issue with Tucker and Axel, but I didn't know how to ask them about their employee without sounding like I was questioning their judgment again. As the three of us had gotten used to one another, we had butted heads less, and I preferred that. I was trusting them a lot more, and I had promised to follow their lead with my safety.

On the fourth night, the cloud cover blew away, and the temperature started dropping uncomfortably. We built up the fire in both stoves as best we could, but we ended up using a milkhouse heater in the horse shed and laying out the memory foam mattresses from the folding beds for all three of us, directly in front of the fire. Even then and with extra quilts and with the men's enormous bodies on either side of me, I still lay there for a good while, too chilly to sleep. When I finally did, I ended up wishing I hadn't.

The ghost bear was back.

The one from the legend, who had once lived here, and he didn't like his shed being repurposed for horses and his cabin full of strangers. I could hear his heavy footsteps crunching through the ice-crusted snow outside, punctuating his low, harsh breathing and occasional growl. He knew I was the new owner. He hated me, way more than just carrying a grudge for my taking his place. For reasons I still didn't fully understand, he wanted me dead. And my guardians with me.

But he was smart. He didn't smash in the door to face two wolves head on. Instead, he used human tools to drive us out to him and pick us off at his leisure. And the one he chose first was the oldest human tool of all.

At first, I thought the crackle and smell came from the stove fires warming the air inside the cabin. But then I saw that the porch was on fire. The roof was glowing in spots, dropping embers down on us. The curtains somehow caught through the glass. Fire spread inside.

We had to get out. But inexplicably, I knew there was an even greater danger waiting for us out there, posed by a much more modern tool.

Face a burning building, or face a bullet?

I tried to warn Tucker and Axel as they dragged me toward the back door. I knew he was waiting out there. The man who had burned my barn created a distraction while trying to put a bullet in my head. But my mouth just wouldn't form the right words.

The door opened. Tucker bulled his way through first, into the swirling snow, and then I heard the gunshot and saw him fall.

I woke up and clapped my hands over my mouth, muffling my shocked cry. I was sitting bolt upright, dizzy from coming out of the dream so fast, the shock and sense of loss so keen that it hurt even after I realized that both men were safe and sound next to me.

They both woke up, Tucker taking longer and stifling a yawn as he propped himself up on one arm. "Nightmare?" he mumbled.

I nodded mutely.

Axel put his hand on my arm. "Pretty bad one, huh?" He sounded worried.

"Uh-huh," I mumbled. "The sniper. He found us. He burned the cabin and was waiting outside with a gun." I started shaking, hugging myself. At least my eyes were still dry.

Axel sat up beside me. "Hey, it's going to be okay." He slid his hand up to my shoulder. Tucker placed a hand on my other arm.

"I know. I just…" Dammit, now my lips were trembling. My eyes were stinging. "What if he finds us?"

What if he burns the place and waits outside to ambush us?

"If he finds us," Tucker said firmly, "we'll make him wish he never fucking had."

"Yes." Axel nodded. "We're wolf-shifters. He's some asshole with a gun. There's no contest. You're safe with us. Trust us."

Before I really thought about it, I turned toward Axel. He pulled me against him, and I curled into his arms. I didn't want to give in, but the strength of him, the warmth of his body against mine, was too seductive.

He set one finger beneath my chin, lifting my face to his. "It's going to be all right, Alina. Trust us."

I wanted to. It seemed like my body already did, because I was tingling all over. But mostly, what I wanted was for the racing thoughts, the misery, the shaking to just go away.

I looked into his eyes, his gaze intense now with something more primal than what I'd seen earlier. My shaking stopped, and I tilted my head back, breathlessly offering my mouth.

He bent his head, catching my lips with his. The kiss was gentle but firm, his lips drifting over mine. A little voice said that this was all kinds of wrong. That I barely knew him. That he wasn't even human, if I wanted to get down to it. But my body didn't care about the voice. All it cared about was the feeling of his lips on mine, his arms around me, the closeness of our bodies. Those sensations pushed back the aloneness, the frightened feeling.

I kissed him back, hard, and the kiss deepened. Axel's hands slid down my back, and I wound my arms around his neck, pulling him even closer. Lips parted, tongues danced, and I let feelings take over from thought.

Cool air shimmied up my back as he tugged on my shirt, fingers skating along my bare skin, caressing my breasts.

Oh God, that's good, except...wait a second...

Something was different. There were too many hands. Math wasn't my strong suit, but Axel's hands on my back and the two on my breasts added Tucker to the equation. I pulled away reluctantly, looking first at Axel and then over my shoulder. *Are they really both...?*

Tucker was kneeling behind me, and as our eyes met, he leaned forward, nuzzling my neck. I tipped my head to the side, closed my eyes, and let the heat of his lips on my skin fan the flame inside me.

The little voice broke through, insistent that this was still wrong, even more wrong to give in to two men I barely knew, much less one. But...

I was staring at the shadowy ceiling, gaze taking in the exposed beams without fastening on them. My heart was beating fast. I closed my eyes, giving in to this. "Fuck it."

"Sorry?" Tucker lifted his head from my neck. He sounded amused.

I realized I must have spoken out loud. "Sorry. Nothing at all. Just—" I looked into Axel's eyes "—making the decision that I want this. But are you two okay with this?"

I caught the glance he gave Tucker over my shoulder. In response, Tucker's hands tightened against me, a silent answer to my question.

"One more thing," I said. "We need to talk about protection. I'm on birth control, and I'm STI-free."

"We're both STI-free," Axel replied. "It's a shifter thing. We don't give or get STIs."

Tucker nodded. "And about the possibility of getting you pregnant, we can scent if you're ovulating. You're not now."

I blinked. "Holy hell. That's a pretty powerful ability."

They both nodded.

"Okay, then... Ravish me, shifters." I leaned back against Tucker, reaching up to run a hand through his hair, turning my head to find his mouth seeking mine.

Our kiss was sexy, lush, and erotic. He thrust his tongue into my mouth, and I sucked on it briefly, wanting to pull him inside my mouth.

Axel moved his hands to my hips, pulling me up to a kneeling position. Tucker rose with me, moving behind me. He broke away from our kiss, and with regret, I let him go.

But Axel was there, his sensuous mouth already capturing mine. He pulled me against him, our bodies meeting, me melting into him. Behind me, Tucker molded himself to me, his chest against my back, the hardness of his hips—and what he held between them—pressed against my ass. I could feel his heart-beat pounding in his chest and groin against my back and ass. Axel, just as fast, was against my belly and breasts.

If the room was still cold, I wasn't. I was on fire, inside and out. I wiggled against both men, which elicited a low moan from Tucker and a smile against my mouth from Axel.

Someone was undoing the buttons on my shirt, and I didn't care who it was. The fabric came away from my body, and I reluctantly let go of Axel as he pulled the shirt down my arms. I shivered, the heat of the fire licking one side of me, the coolness of the room raising goose bumps on the other. And their heat, sinking into me from front and back.

Axel pulled away, looking down between us. It was his hands that rose now, cupping my breasts, fingers sliding over my simple white cotton bra.

I whimpered softly, watching his hands as he caressed me, pushing my breasts together, leaning forward to run his tongue over my exposed skin and down in between, nimbly probing every inch of my cleavage. He moved between my breasts, lavishing kisses on them.

Tucker was kissing a line along my shoulder, fingers working at the clasp of my bra. It came undone, and he slowly pulled first one and then the other bra strap down my arms. I let him manipulate me, let him move my arms, until the only thing holding the bra against my breasts was Axel's hands.

He raised his head and pulled the bra away, dropping it out of sight. Between the chill and my arousal, my nipples drew up hard and tight. Axel leaned in again, this time pushing me back against Tucker, licking and sucking at my breasts, my nipples. It overwhelmed my nerves, making me whimper and moan, my nipples so hard they almost hurt. I wound my fingers through his hair, holding him against me. "Oh God..."

Tucker eased me down onto my back, Axel breaking away from me with a gasp. I looked up at them, these two men so totally different in looks, in manners, but now both focused on me, on wherever this was going next.

I had never had a threesome in my life.

I had never even fantasized about being shared by two men. Outside of ridiculous proposals by horny college boyfriends and idiots on dating sites, the concept just had never entered my mind.

But here it was happening, and I wanted it. So bad that I couldn't seem to catch my breath.

Axel knelt between my knees, and the bulge at the front of his jeans was unmistakable. So was the shake in his breath. He reached for the snap and zipper on my jeans, and I let him pull them down over my hips, tugging them off me. Beneath me, the thick rug was as sensual as any satin sheets, and I wiggled deeper into it. I felt giddy and excited and deeply aroused.

Throbbing had begun low in my belly, a subtle tensing and fluttering of places inside me that hadn't stirred in far too long. Even though it was winter outside, I felt like something awakening in the spring, blossoming, coming alive. And I loved every minute.

How long had it been? I couldn't even remember. But I knew that sex had never been this intoxicating, this tempting, before now...and the two of them.

Tucker moved away, throwing another log onto the fire. He came back to me, lying beside me, pulling me against him roughly. He kissed me hard, reaching down to cup my ass, his fingers sliding lower, teasing the heat between my legs. Without hesitation, I slid one thigh over his jean-clad leg, opening myself to him, letting him find his way to the spot that desperately needed his touch. I felt like I might climax with just a few more caresses, but I doubted even that would leave me satisfied. I wanted both of them. Every inch of them pressed against me, sliding into me.

At my back, I felt Axel's warmth before I felt the touch of his hands on my skin, his soft lips on my neck. Tucker released me reluctantly, almost as though it pained him to share. I moved toward Axel and discovered he was gloriously naked. My mouth missed his, sliding instead down his throat, into that wonderful hollow at the base of his neck, where his pulse beat against my lips.

He pulled me into his arms, and I went willingly. My breasts pressed to his hard chest, my taut nipples brushing against his, sending prickly little jolts through me. I felt the throbbing head of his cock slide against my belly. He lifted my face to his and claimed my mouth, crushing his lips to mine, stealing my breath away.

There were hands on me again, and Axel lifted me up to my feet, before easing me onto my back, rising over me, his chest pressing me into the mattress of the camp bed. My heart had been pounding in my ears so hard that I hadn't even heard them pull it down. He kissed me harder, and I gave back just as much, just as hard, matching his passion, lust, and desire with my own.

The fear faded, the stress and tension falling away as Axel's hands roamed over my body, cradling my head, sliding down my back, pulling my thigh over his hip. Warmth from the fire played over the most intimate part of me, leaving me gasping for air as their onslaught tortured my senses, leaving me wild with a hunger I was desperate to satisfy.

Then there were hands on my breasts again, warmer than the fire, probing, testing, exciting me deeply. I broke the kiss, looking over my shoulder at Tucker, down over what I could see of him, and I could see that he, too, was naked. The thought crossed my mind that they got undressed quickly, and I wondered if that had anything to do with being a shifter. If it was, it was a pretty handy skill to have at a time like this, when our bodies begged for the heat of one another. When we felt chilled to the bone the moment we moved away from the scorching lust of a lover's touch.

But then Axel turned my head, kissing me, and I lost my train of thought, letting him guide me to a thoughtless place of no return. A place I had secretly longed to go for so very long, yet never imagined I'd ever experience. Total sensual abandon. I no longer cared about the aftermath of this, when the cold of late winter and the people gunning for me would creep back into my mind. Those kinds of thoughts now belonged to a whole other world.

Axel pressed himself against me, the whole naked length of him hard and hot, and it was beyond erotic. They sandwiched me between them. Men who were *strangers* and wolf-shifters. Men with whom I had spent most of my time out of bed butting heads ever since they had arrived.

For a minute, I faltered in my kiss, turning away from Axel, amazed and shocked at what I was doing. At how easy it seemed to be in the arms of these two impossibly gorgeous, yet all-too-mysterious men.

"What's wrong?" Axel set a finger under my chin, tipping my face to his. Those dark eyes held mine, and I searched them for something that would tell me this was okay, that I didn't have to be afraid of this or them or anything.

"I don't normally do this." I shrugged, and Tucker's lips were on my shoulder. "It feels kinky and taboo, like maybe I shouldn't want this."

Axel just smiled teasingly. But Tucker chuckled in my ear and murmured, "But you want this."

I turned my head and scowled. "You know nothing about me. I..." But before I could say anything else, he rose, kissing me hard. When he broke away, I was breathless, all thought of protest lost in the kiss, and I was ready to surrender.

Tucker was smirking. "You know, you talk too damn much sometimes."

I snorted a laugh and smiled. "So, shut me up, then."

After that, there were no more words, only the sounds of us, of our kisses, gasps, and deep moans of satisfaction.

Axel rolled onto his back, greedily taking me with him. I lay on top of him, my breasts pressed against his chest, our lips and tongues exploring each other. He was intoxicating and arousing, his dark eyes catching the light from the fire.

I sat up, straddling his hips, the shaft of his erection sliding between my legs. I wanted him, more than I could have thought possible, considering who he was and where we were. His cock was so hot and throbbing, and I wanted to claim it. It belonged only to me. *At least for this moment in time.*

It all seemed right. I took him in my hand, guiding him into me. He grabbed my hips, easing me down onto his erection, and I gasped as he entered me, not allowing me to take my time. He took control wordlessly, forcing me down onto him, my pussy stretching as though I had never had a lover before, until he was as deep inside me as he could ever be.

"Oh my God!" I groaned, and I felt my body tremble as he thrust his hips in time with mine, my body bouncing up and down on top of his throbbing cock.

Tucker came up behind me, wrapping his arms around me, hands on my torso. He cupped my breasts, caressing them in his hands, rolling my nipples between his fingers. I reached up, hands in his hair as though it were the reins of a horse, as I struggled to stay on this wild and intoxicating ride.

Beneath me, Axel began thrusting upward, fingers digging into my hips. I rode him easily, bracing my knees on the mattress. He'd never know how lucky he was, what years of riding a horse did to a woman's thigh muscles. I was strong, and I loved the feel of my body as I moved and shifted, rising, coming down on him, grinding against him. Apparently, he loved it too. I caught his grin, the approval in his eyes.

"You feel so fucking good," he growled, his teeth clenched, his jaw firm.

Tucker turned my head to him, kissing me hard, his tongue darting into my mouth. One hand left my breast, moving down my stomach, slipping between my legs. He hit the jackpot, fingers brushing against my swollen clit. I jerked, crying out. Hearing his low chuckle rumbling in my ear added one more sensation to this already rich mix of pleasure.

I let Tucker hold me while I rode Axel wildly, every thrust bringing me closer to the edge. Everything within me was a maelstrom of emotion and sensation, growing hotter, more intense. I gave in, gave up trying to think, let my body tell me what it wanted, let Axel and Tucker guide me wherever they wished for me to go.

It was the perfect storm, and everything suddenly flashed over, leaving me aching with an almost painful need for release. I bucked hard, arching against Tucker, his hands holding me as I rocked and shuddered, my legs splayed over Axel. Beneath me, he jerked, his cock thrusting into me, filling me up completely, and I felt his hot seed explode inside me, marking his territory. He came with a deep growl, his warmth heating me up inside. I felt each pulse of him inside me, matching my own internal quivering, and I wanted to scream out as I rode the wave of pleasure.

Before I was really aware of what was happening, Tucker pulled me back, and I slid in an almost boneless heap onto the bed. He knelt between my legs, pulling me by the hips up between his thighs. I looked up, into eyes alive with lust and desire, and then down to his erection, already sliding into my heated body.

Just the touch of him set everything in me alive again, and I screamed as he thrust home. Axel leaned over, kissing me, and I took him wantonly. Tucker pulled me farther up his thighs, holding me easily, thrusting hard.

"Oh, Alina... You are so damn beautiful. So damn hot."

He came quickly, head back, a growl rippling from his throat. I was so lost in my own swirling orgasm, I only heard him, was dimly aware of him bucking into me. I closed my eyes and gave in to the seductive pleasure.

Axel was cradling my head, Tucker lying beside me. "Hey..." He brushed a strand of hair away from my face. "You okay?"

I turned to look at him. "I'm better than I've ever been." I managed a smile. My body felt equal parts leaden and light, and I was having a hard time telling where I ended and the warmth of the flames started. All I wanted was sleep, to curl up with these beautiful men, and to put everything else behind me, at least for a few hours.

I turned toward Axel, and Tucker molded himself against my back. The fire kissed our bodies, and I listened to the breathing of these two. I drifted for a while, feeling safe for the first time in a very long time.

$$\text{❧} \quad 9 \quad \text{☙}$$

I woke up completely disoriented. The fire was low, just glowing embers left, and the windows were dark. Someone had covered me with the afghan, and I pulled it around my shoulders. From beneath the blanket, the warm, rich scent of sex rose around me. In that moment, it all came back to me. The amazing, mind-blowing sex with *both* of them. I sat up, clutching the afghan to my chest, looking wildly around the empty room.

What the hell had I done?

"Easy, Alina."

I jerked around, staring into the semidarkness. Tucker emerged from the shadows beside the window.

My eyes widened at a dressed Tucker holding a pistol. As he walked into the glow of the fire, I saw the worried look in his eyes.

"What is it? Where's Axel?"

He stood over the fire. For being as good at his job as he claimed, he wasn't very good at hiding his body language. Every muscle was tense, every sense on alert. I struggled to my knees, rooting around on the floor for my clothes.

"You're fine, Alina. Axel heard a noise, went to check. He'll be right back."

I pulled on my shirt, forgoing the buttons for pulling on my jeans. Screw the underwear. *If I was being ambushed, did I really care if I was going commando?*

"Alina, calm down. It's nothing. I'm sure of it. Axel wanted to make sure, though."

"If Axel wanted to make sure, then it's something. And it doesn't take much to see you don't think it's nothing either." I stood up, pulling my jeans all the way on, my hands shaking as I pulled up the zipper. "You need not sugarcoat any of this."

"Fine. He heard a noise. Might have been an animal or one horse that got out of the shed." He shrugged, and in that shrug, I read all I needed to know.

"Someone followed us. You guys found footprints. Or something."

Tucker finally met my eyes. "Always a possibility. We left a pretty obvious trail. And..." He pushed away from the fireplace, crossing to where I stood, barefoot, shirt unbuttoned. "We didn't follow plans."

"I thought spontaneity was the key to a good operation—or whatever you call this." My socks were nowhere in sight. *Fuck it.* I thrust my feet into my cold, wet boots. Though, it bothered me immensely that I couldn't remember when my socks had come off.

"Alina, there's spontaneity, and there's turning the entire operation inside out. We did that." I couldn't tell if he was talking about the trip up to the cabin or the sex, and I didn't ask.

He reached out, brushing back the hair from my face. I swatted at his hand. Playing nice wasn't what I wanted from him now. I wanted the truth; I wanted action. Or lack of action. Or for Axel to come back and tell us it was a bear or a wolf.

"How do you stand this? This limbo of not knowing what's going on." I paced across the room. Three strides took me from the couch to the kitchen, and three strides brought me back to Tucker.

"It comes with practice. You learn to be patient. Rushing out, rushing ahead, or pushing the issue just makes things worse. You learn to wait, to listen. To be still."

He reached out and pulled me against him. I went, but reluctantly. I wanted to know there was no one outside with a rifle trained on my back. He held me, and the fire warmed my legs. I listened, harder than I ever had, harder than I did when I was a kid, waiting for my parents to come back from some fund raiser, waiting to hear the rumble of the garage door, feeling that only then was I safe from whatever was out there.

I hadn't really known then that being the relative of an influential politician could be physically dangerous. Not consciously. But I sure as hell did now.

We were still standing in front of the fire when the door opened and Axel came in from the cold. I turned, glimpsing the dark world outside the door before he slammed it shut. Apparently, the snow had started up again while I had slept off all that sex. His dark hair and jacket were lightly dusted with snow. He glanced at me, then Tucker.

"Tracks. Only one. Came up the trail, circled the cabin, then went back. I followed them back down the trail, and they cut off into the woods." He took off his jacket and hung it up.

"What else? You guys are horrible at keeping things secret. Just say it." I looked between the two men.

Axel looked at me, took a step forward and then stopped. He ran a hand through his hair, the thick, dark strands tangling in his fingers.

"The tracks weren't human, or not all of them. There were wolf tracks. Whoever it is, it's a shifter."

* * *

They were pacing, and I was sitting on the couch. I waited for Axel to explain what this meant, if it meant anything. *Could it be the wolves from town? Had Shamus gone off the rails completely?*

"It means we need to rethink staying here. Whoever found

us did so because they're a shifter. They tracked us here by scent. They know where we are, and that's as good as..."

"That's as good as me being dead." I had the overwhelming urge to pull the afghan over my head. That old childhood "if I can't see them, they can't see me" trick. Comforting, but not all that effective.

"We can't do anything now. It's pitch-black, and there's a foot of new snow on the trail."

"So, we're sitting ducks? Waiting for the sniper slash arsonist to strike again?" I pulled my knees up to my chest, wrapping my arms around them. The room was warm, but my teeth were chattering. That dream kept running through my head. It seemed closer to a real possibility than just a nightmare now.

Tucker sat down beside me, and Axel hunkered down in front of me. I looked pointedly at the gun in Axel's hand, but all I got in response was a cocked eyebrow.

"Listen. This happens sometimes. We diverged from our plan, followed yours," Tucker started.

I thought I caught a note of recrimination and started to answer, but Tucker held up his hand.

"It doesn't matter. It could have—probably would have—happened, no matter where we went. You've got to understand that shifters operate on a whole different level from..."

"From humans?" I couldn't help the smartass comment. But when I saw the look in Tucker's eyes, I regretted my words. "I'm sorry. That was mean."

Axel took my hand into his. "Alina, you're in a situation that's beyond anything you could have imagined. A few snarky comments will not bother us."

I glanced at him, then back at Tucker. I wasn't so sure about that, but right now, I was more interested in saving my own life than about Tucker's feelings.

Tucker kept his cool. "We'll keep watch, like we have been. You can try to get some sleep, but I have a feeling you won't. One of us will make a circuit outside every so often. If we see anything, we'll let you know. And we'll decide at first light what to do. Right now, the general thought is that we'll leave then and head back down to the ranch."

Axel looked thoughtful. "Is there another trail back to the valley? Some other way down the mountain than the way we came?"

I shook my head, but then some distant corner of my mind spoke up. "There's something I remember. From the ghost story...not the ghost part, but from the actual lore of the area." I sat up, pulling my hand away from Axel's so I could talk with both hands.

"We're here..." I drew a circle in the air. "We came up this way." I drew an imaginary trail up to the circle with my right hand.

"Where we are now, is on the side of the mountain, perched more or less on a flat spot, but not really a valley. There's been rumor of a trail that goes up, around, and then back down." I made a spiral motion, bringing my hand back down to where the ranch would be. "It follows various gold claims up the mountain. I know hunters come up here without passing by my ranch. That might be how they're getting here. So, in theory, there's another way down from here." I hoped.

"Have you seen this trail? Or has Henry?" Axel leaned forward, eyes pinned on mine.

"No. Like I said, it's just a rumor. The reason Ezra's killer friend could get from Point A to Point B without being seen."

Tucker looked up at Axel. "Head out that way, see what you can find. If there's anything that remotely resembles a trail, even if it's an animal trail, we'll take it."

"Will do." Axel rose, then looked back at me. There was a strange hesitation in his look, in his posture, and a lot of words not being said.

"What? More surprises?" I sat back, my already-frayed nerves unraveling a little more.

"I want to go out as a wolf... It's easier for me to look around.

I want to shift. But..." He shrugged, looking equal parts unsure and cocky.

"Well, don't hold back on my account." Behind that bravado was a healthy dose of alarm and uncertainty. I did not understand what shifting entailed, other than at the end, I suspected a really gigantic wolf was going to be in my cabin.

"It can be a bit...overwhelming if you haven't seen it."

"How the hell would I prepare for something like this?" I stood up, hands on hips. "My life has taken a bunch of sharp left turns in the last week. This will probably be one of the tamer ones." I heard Tucker's laugh behind me and turned around. "What's so funny?"

"Your reaction. You're such a little spitfire." He held up one hand. "And yes, that's a compliment. Really. But Axel's right. For a shifter virgin, seeing someone change for the first time can be pretty raw. Especially someone you've seen in, shall we say, a different light."

He had the grace to look away before the blush I felt reached full volume. I turned away from both of them, waving a hand in Axel's general direction.

"Fine. Do what you have to do. I'll be over here, in the human corner."

I heard the sounds of Axel undressing, and part of my mind came alive, reliving last night, the glow of the fire on his skin, the feel of him beneath my hands. I closed my eyes and gritted my teeth. All that was in the past.

The sounds changed, and it filled the room with an eerie noise, half-human, mostly animal, and I couldn't help but turn around and watch.

Axel stood in the center of the room, muscles taut, head back. His sleek swimmer's body thickened, arms and legs bulking up, his chest swelling.

I took an involuntary step forward, bumping into Tucker. He wrapped an arm around my waist, holding me, either from going forward or cowering back. I snuggled up against him and held my breath.

Axel's breathing sped up and got raspy and harsh. Beneath that was another sound, an unmistakable growl, deep and resonant, almost too low to hear. I felt it in my chest, though, along with the thudding of my heart.

There was a moment of stillness, a strange anticipation. Then all hell broke loose. Axel dropped to the floor, the growl overlaid by a scream. It tore through me like a devil wind and sent my senses reeling. I'd heard a version of that scream last night, as we'd brought one another to the edge of oblivion. There had been more pleasure than pain in that sound last night. Not this time.

I blinked, and there was a massive white wolf shaking its magnificent head, almost glowing in the fire's light. The wolf—Axel—looked up at me with steady silver eyes. That was the last thing I remembered, because the next moment, I fainted.

❦ 10 ❦

"Alina? Hey...wake up."

I opened my eyes. Tucker was sitting on the edge of the couch, holding my hand. I blinked, then sat up, almost knocking heads with him.

"Slow down. You're fine."

"He changed into a wolf. I saw it." I looked past Tucker, but the room was empty, just Axel's clothes draped across the chair. "I said I could handle it, and then I fainted."

"You did. I told you it could be a little much." He reached up and smoothed a strand of hair away from my face.

"Does that hurt?" I blurted out the first thing that came to my mind. "He screamed..."

Tucker gave me a wry smile. "That may have been some theatrics on his part. It's not painful, like a broken bone or a cut. It's just really intense. There's no actual way to give you anything to compare it to." Tucker looked into the fire. It was blazing now. He must have added a log or two.

"It's probably the most exhilarating feeling I can think of. Aside from sex." He gave me a sidelong glance, lip quirking upward. "It's a close second."

"Did you start out this way, or did something happen?" I

wasn't quite sure if I wanted to ask if he'd had an accident or if it was magic or whatever the hell it was.

"I was born as a shifter. My pack has all been wolves for as far back as we can remember. Axel's the same. Our parents are shifters, their parents. It's in the blood."

"But you went to school with humans? How do you function in a human world?"

Tucker laughed, shaking his head. "Okay. You want a mini history lesson about my life." He sat back against the couch cushions, and I curled up against the arm, wrapping the afghan around my legs. The chill had returned to the cabin while we'd slept, and the fire had yet to push it back.

"I grew up in an upper-middle-class Chicago family. I went to school, just like everyone else did. Graduated near the top of my class in high school, then went to an Ivy League college. Joined the Marines and ended up serving in the Middle East. I met Axel on my last tour."

He was quiet a minute, and I thought there was a lot more to his life history than the synopsis I was getting. I tried to hold back the million questions I had and waited for him to go on.

"We hit it off really well, became fast friends. People have confused us for brothers on more than one occasion." He looked at me, chuckled briefly and continued on. "Although you are the first to think we're gay."

"Oh well. You used the word 'partner' and all... Cut me some slack. I'd had a bad day."

He reached out and rubbed my knee. "It's okay. Anyway, after we got back to the States, neither of us knew what we wanted to do. Jobs were scarce, the recession hit, the economy... You know the story."

I did. "So, you ended up working together?"

"We found an agency, Lockhart's, run by a man named Lyndon Kingsley." Tucker stared into the fire, his gaze distant, voice going low.

"Lockhart's was a bodyguard-for-hire agency, but the twist

was they used shifters like us. For the first time in a long time, I felt like I was someplace where I could be myself. I didn't have to hide being a shifter. Lockhart's was a place that valued what I was, and I could use it to my advantage."

"It must have been hard, overseas in the military, being a shifter." I thought it must have been pretty close to impossible.

"It was a challenge. But I learned more over there than I ever could have back in the States. My father is a lawyer, and let's say, he's had me pegged to take over the firm since before I was born."

I couldn't help but laugh. "Your father and mine must be related. He's... Well, you know who he is. He wanted me to follow in his impossibly large footsteps forever. Either become a politician or marry one. I didn't want to do either. I wasn't interested in politics and didn't have the stomach for it."

Tucker shot me a look, and I beat him to the punch line. "Even if I have the temperament and personality for it. I can't play the games, can't stand the backstabbing or glad-handing. All the shit that goes along with the job. And I sure as hell can't stand marrying some asshole friend of my father's who is twice my age."

I sat back in a huff. "Yet, here I am, stuck in a cabin with a target on my back because of being my father's daughter."

We watched the fire for a while, in a silence that was more comforting than not. It felt good to rail against my father, even if I was preaching to the choir.

"Shouldn't Axel be back by now?" I looked at the window. It was still dark outside, but I figured it wasn't too long before it would start getting light.

"He went to look for the trail. I'm pretty confident he can handle himself against anything he finds out there—man, beast, or shifter." But Tucker's tensed muscles said more than his words.

"Are you going to go look for him?"

He turned to me, and I smiled. "I can read people pretty well, Tucker. You're worried."

"I'm cautious." But he rose anyway and went to the window, standing to the side and peering out past the gingham curtain. "You know what... You're right. Ten more minutes, and then I'll make a run out. I don't want to leave you alone, though."

"I can handle myself. Just leave me a gun."

Tucker chuckled. "I guess that request shouldn't surprise me." Then he stiffened, and I tensed, waiting for the worst.

The door of the cabin opened, and Axel almost fell into the room in human form. He was naked, and I jumped up off the couch, throwing the blanket around him, pulling him down to the fire.

"Axel! What the hell?" Tucker crouched down beside us. Axel's teeth were chattering, but he spoke.

"I found it. I found the trail down the back of the mountain."

$\maltese$ I I $\maltese$

Light was filtering through the window by the time Axel finished telling us what had happened. Tucker had pulled a flask from his pack, and from the aroma, I could tell whatever was in it was a hell of a lot stronger than the whiskey we'd shared after our hike up. Axel took a long swallow, blinked, and then drained the flask.

"He's a wolf-shifter, just the one. I don't think he's from here, though, and he's not a professional. He followed our trail, but after that, he seemed lost, tentative, almost like he blundered on us by accident. Maybe the snowstorm disoriented him, though really, it was more wind than flakes. The crust on the snow from earlier held his footprints. He circled the cabin twice last night but never made a move, then he went back the way he came."

"You think if he was local, he'd have knocked on the door and introduced himself?" I scowled at Axel as I pulled the afghan more tightly around his shoulders.

"No. I mean, that if he was familiar with the area, he might have been more careful in covering his tracks, not taking the trail right to our door. He'd have watched, waited, and made a move when he was sure of his target."

"You mean me." I sat back, deciding that fussing over a grown man was silly.

"I mean, it's how Tucker or I would have behaved. This guy isn't local, doesn't know his way around the mountains, and we were lucky." Axel pulled the afghan off, freeing his arms. The blanket fell away from his body, and the firelight licked at his chest and arms. I hated that I noticed all of that and sat back, putting space between us.

"But I found the trail out, down the backside of the mountain. I want to get going before he comes back and sees the tracks I left. There's no way I could cover them. The snow is too deep, and the wind's died. I tried to make it look accidental, haphazard, but almost anyone could follow where I went."

Tucker took back his flask and stood. "Then let's get moving. Can the horses handle the trail?"

Axel stood, and the afghan fell farther down his body. Almost as an afterthought, he grabbed it, saving the last bit of my sanity. He was too goddamn beautiful, and despite the craziness going on, just catching sight of the trimmed hairs below his belly reminded me of our wild night together. I wanted to forget that, especially right now. I had to focus.

"If we're careful, and you break the trail with that big black horse, I think we'll be okay." He turned to look down at me. "Get your stuff, and let's go." He held out a hand, and I took it, letting him pull me to my feet, then closer to him. He radiated heat and something else, a primal animal magnetism that took my breath away. "Were you worried about me?"

"Yes."

"Thank you for caring." He touched my cheek. "And I'm sorry if I scared you when I shifted. It's a pretty compelling visual."

"That's for sure."

He smiled and let the blanket fall to the floor. The look he gave me was equal parts confident and cocky.

I went from cold with fear to burning hot in seconds.

"Okay. Put it away, Axel. We're in a bit of a rush here." Tucker was moving around the cabin, packing up the few things he'd taken out of his pack. Axel threw him a look, then reached for his clothes. His eyes never left mine as he pulled on his jeans and then his t-shirt. By the time he got dressed, I was ten degrees hotter. I reached for my underwear, which was the only thing of mine left on the floor.

I grabbed my pack, stuffed them unceremoniously inside, and turned to the guys. "Ready." I reached for the door handle, but I'd only got the door open a few inches when a whistling sound filled the air, and the doorframe splintered around me, sending wood fragments everywhere. Axel made a dive for me, pushing me to the floor and slamming the door behind us.

"I thought you said he wasn't a professional." I lay gasping beneath Axel. "That had all the earmarks of a high-powered rifle being shot at my head."

"If he were a professional, he wouldn't have missed." But Axel didn't sound entirely convinced. He pushed himself off me, crouching low. Tucker was in motion too, ducking below the level of the window.

"You think he's expecting two of us?" Tucker twitched the curtain aside, looking out. His face was grim, and I tried to remember if my will gave the ranch to Henry or Dad. It had to be Henry. I wouldn't have slipped enough in my judgment to give my land to someone who badmouthed it every chance he got.

"He's only seen one of us outside, but there are three sets of horse tracks," Axel replied. "Can't tell if he'd think that's three people or someone coming up with a packhorse."

Tucker's familiar growl came from the other side of the room. "If he knew his business, he'd know to read the depth of the tracks." He sat back against the wall. "I say we divide and conquer. I'll get the horses. You get the sniper."

Axel nodded, grabbing his jacket, pulling a small silver pistol from the pocket. He checked the rounds and nodded. "I'm on it. Cover me." He crouched by the door, opened it, and made a dash, not toward the shed, but off the other side of the porch. I reached up, pulling the door shut as another shot rang out.

"Was he hit?" I looked in alarm at Tucker. He had his back to me, looking out the window.

"No. I see him in the woods. He's circling around where the sniper is. We need to wait a minute."

A minute seemed like an eternity. But then in the distance, I heard a pop, different from the rifle shot. Tucker nodded, watched another minute, then turned to me.

"Let's go." He stood up, crossed the room in three strides, and pulled me up from the floor. I stumbled up after him, my pack left behind. But it was the last thing I cared about. I wanted to see Axel, I wanted to get the horses, I wanted to go home.

Tucker ran the short distance to the shed, me on his heels. He yanked open the door. Tucker grabbed Storm's saddle as I moved for Jane's, throwing a blanket across her back, then yanking the saddle off the rack, setting it on the horse. I'd gotten the blanket on Mary and was reaching for her saddle when the shed door opened. Axel slipped inside.

"I shot him. But I don't think one silver bullet will do the job, and he may not be working alone. We should be able to make it back, if we get going."

We finished saddling the horses, leading them outside. Storm tossed his head, pulling against Tucker, who gave the bridle a sharp tug. The horse settled.

We went the other direction from the trail we'd taken. I turned to Axel. "We're still taking this trail?"

"We are. If he had a partner, then he's probably expecting us to use the same path down we took up here. It's clear he doesn't know about this trail, so he won't expect us to know about it either."

There was something in his tone that made the hair rise on the back of my neck. "But there's more, right? There's always more."

"Any backup he has will come looking for him if they heard the shots. And when he finds us gone, all he has to do is follow our tracks. Our only advantage now is getting the hell off the mountain as fast as we can. And watching our backs."

That wasn't the most reassuring thing I'd heard, but there didn't seem to be a choice. I climbed up on Mary. Tucker was already astride Storm. I turned just in time to see Axel trying to climb onto Jane.

He winced, his leg giving out as he pushed up from the ground and clambered into the saddle. He got settled, then caught my gaze, scowling.

"I'm fine. Don't worry about me." He brought the horse around, and as he did, I saw a dark stain on his jeans.

"You're bleeding," I whispered. Mary danced past Jane, and I pulled her up hard, swinging her around. Axel and I were side by side.

"It's fine." A muscle twitched in his jaw, and his eyes went dark and hard. "Just a flesh wound. He's not even loading silver."

"Flesh wound. Right." I leaned toward him. "Stop being a tough guy for a minute and level with me. Are you okay?"

His look softened, but barely. "I'm okay to get off this mountain. You pay attention to getting yourself down, and we'll worry about me later."

"What's the holdup?" Tucker had ridden a few yards ahead. "We need to get moving."

Axel nodded in Tucker's direction. "We're ready. Let's go." He brought his gaze back to me, and I saw there was no reasoning—or arguing—with the man. I turned Mary's head and nudged her forward, following Tucker as Storm broke the trail.

I'd never gone past the cabin, never climbed higher up the mountain. And even though I could see Axel's tracks and had been told there was a trail, what we were following seemed more like just a wide space between the trees.

We climbed up the backside of the mountain, through the pines, and through deeper and deeper snow. The storm had blasted this side of the mountain, and the drifts in the clearings were growing taller. I knew Storm would keep going as long as someone riding him was in control, and I hoped Tucker was that someone. Because if Storm decided it was a no-go, then we were all stuck between a snowdrift and a sniper.

Tucker held tight to the horse's reins, keeping him from balking. The snowbanks broke against his broad strides, cutting a path for the rest of us. I lost track of time, focusing on keeping Mary heading in the right direction and not stumbling into deeper snow. Flakes had fallen from the sky again, and I prayed it wouldn't turn into another whiteout.

When I finally looked away from Storm's rear end, I realized we were heading down the other side of the mountain. I could see down into the pasture belonging to Jess Montgomery. His big beef cattle looked small from here, but seeing their shaggy black forms lifted my heart. I'd never been so happy to see a cow before and turned back with an excited grin to tell Axel.

But I caught a movement in the trees behind Axel, a large shape moving fast. I pulled Mary up short. Axel looked up, caught my gaze, and his brows drew down. He swiveled in the saddle, scanning the thick pines, then he jumped off the horse. Jane snorted and tossed her head, and I struggled to turn Mary around, slogging back to grab Jane's reins.

Axel disappeared into the woods, moving impossibly easily through the snow. I rose in the saddle, scanning the dark undergrowth, but he'd vanished.

"Tucker..." I sat down, turning back. But before I could say anything else, Mary snorted, tossed her head, and sidestepped almost off the broken path. As I fought for control, another shape moved past me, this time clearly visible. It was another wolf, this one as dark as a thundercloud.

It was Tucker.

❧ 1 2 ☙

For a minute, I was in the middle of a maelstrom of panicked horses. I slid off Mary, holding the reins, making an effort not to drop Jane's. Storm was snorting and prancing a few feet away, and I managed to half pull, half drag myself and the fillies toward him.

"Storm. Calm down." I used my best *I'm-in-charge* voice, and I got his attention long enough to grab the reins. By then, I was standing in a fairly well-trampled circle of snow, and maneuvering the horses got a little easier.

"It's okay. It's fine, big guy." I stroked Storm's neck, and he tossed his head, but he had stopped tugging at the reins. At that point, I think the words were more for my comfort than his, and I repeated them like a mantra.

A sudden roar from the edge of the trees brought all our heads around. There was another low growl, and a vaguely familiar gigantic gray-and-brown wolf crashed down out of the pines, closely followed by the mismatched forms of Axel and Tucker. I blinked and willed myself not to bolt down the side of the mountain.

Tucker and Axel moved around the stranger, circling it on the trail. The stranger wolf snarled and snapped at them, but they moved with ease out of its way. The white one favored a hind leg, which left faint, rusty stains on the snow.

The lone wolf, bigger than either of them, raised its hackles, and its snarl turned into something like a roar. I cringed, struggling to calm the dancing horses. I'd seen deer killed by wolves, and I shivered at the thought of what those claws and teeth could do to me, or Axel and Tucker.

Axel circled in front of the stranger, his weakness even more clear, almost dragging his leg behind him. He was tiring, probably from the blood loss. He snarled at my would-be killer, ears back, fangs exposed. He crouched, and I watched in horror as he prepared to lunge.

The stranger had eyes only for Axel, and I could see the predatory glint as it looked at him. It roared again, front legs spread wide, and came at him.

I screamed as the killer charged. Axel stayed in a crouch, eyes locked on the animal. I expected him to do something, anything, but he remained where he was. His injury must have been far more serious than I'd realized. I just hoped he and Tucker had a plan to compensate for it. *I trust you. Just please...don't die.*

The stranger was within inches of Axel, its slavering jaws almost in his face, when Tucker hit the beast from its blindside. The impact rolled the larger wolf onto its side, away from Axel. In that instant, Axel was up, hurtling himself into the stranger, sinking his fangs into the fur around its neck.

Tucker caught the fur and loose skin of its hackles and held on, pulling and twisting as he bit deeper. The lone wolf howled in rage and pain, throwing its head back and forth to dislodge Tucker, jaws snapping inches away from the dark wolf's head.

Axel released his grip and relaunched himself, body stretched full length, landing on the strange wolf's back, then slid his mouth to bite the stranger on the head, one fang piercing its eye. The wolf screamed, an almost human sound, and I had to look away. The roars of pain went on, the grunts and snarls of Axel and Tucker almost drowned out by them.

I peeked around the edge of Mary's neck, wishing I had a gun but knowing I wasn't anywhere near good enough to kill a wolf with one shot, especially without risking hitting Tucker or Axel. All I could do was watch and pray and try to keep the panicky horses calm.

They were on the ground now, Tucker and Axel going for the kill. Our enemy weakened, but not dead. It thrashed, but the combined weight of the pair kept it from rising. Tucker broke his grip on the neck, changing the angle of his body as the strange wolf struggled beneath him. He rode the larger wolf like a bucking bronco, waiting for his opening. Then he struck, as fast as any rattler, sinking his fangs into the wolf's neck. There was a huge gout of blood, brighter than I'd have thought possible, staining the snow a bold crimson.

The strange wolf's scream changed into a low gurgle as more blood flowed onto the snow. The pair held on, Tucker's face and chest covered in the stranger's blood. Axel leaped off, crouching close, but breathing hard. I saw fresh blood on his leg, and I was pretty sure it was his and not the wolf's.

Tucker gave one final savage twist, and the strange wolf's eye went closed, its head rolling on the snow. He broke away with a snarl but stayed on the prone figure, lips pulled back, bloody teeth exposed. The blood flowed more slowly, the gigantic body going limp. The stranger was dying.

I drew a shuddering breath. These were the men I'd slept with just the night before, and now they'd killed a wolf—no, they'd killed a *man*. The man who had wanted to kill me. I closed my eyes, fighting to calm my racing heart.

"Alina…"

I jumped, striking out, hitting Axel in the chest. Cat-reflex-quick, he grabbed my fist before I could swing again.

"Alina. It's me…Axel."

I stared up at him. He stood naked in front of me, snow swirling around his head. "Don't you ever get cold?"

"Are you going to hit me again?" He still held my hand, and I attempted to unclench my fist.

"No. You startled me... More like, scared the hell out of me." He let go of me, and I took back my hand. "After that..." I closed my eyes, pointing behind him.

There was no answer. I felt a tug on the reins in my hand and opened my eyes. Axel had Jane's bridle, petting her neck, whispering to her. He opened his pack and pulled out sweats and a shirt.

"You go through a lot of clothes being a shifter, don't you?"

I watched him pull on the clothes. He kicked through the snow for a minute, and I realized he was looking for his boots. He found them, glancing up at me as he pulled them on. "Yes. Comes with the territory. Occupational hazard."

"Is he..." I waved my hand in the general direction of the body of the wolf. "Gone?"

"Yeah. He's gone."

"Is he the one who shot at me?"

Axel straightened and took the reins from me. "The caliber of the gun he had was the same they found at the ranch, and the same from the cabin."

"He's the one. He has to be."

We both turned. Tucker was walking toward us, his neck and chest streaked with blood. I looked away, pushing aside a totally inappropriate surge of desire. I heard him moving around behind me, apparently getting dressed.

"We should go." Tucker sounded exhausted.

I looked up at a now-dressed Tucker. He grabbed Storm's reins and mounted the horse. I mounted Mary and saw a patch of snow at the side of the trail, pink with blood. Tucker must have tried to scrub the blood from himself.

The horses were almost wild for the rest of the ride down. The smell of predators and blood was too much for them. I wasn't far off from unhinged myself. The entire morning had been like a nightmare.

The snow was falling now, not backed by the howling wind of last night but coming straight out of the sky in big flakes. It was pretty down in the valley, but I could barely look at it. I had my eyes on the backside of my little woods, the strip that separated my land from Jess Montgomery's pastures.

We crossed the field, the big cattle looking at us curiously. Then they must have caught the scent of blood on the guys. They snorted, tossing their heads, eyes rolling white. Turning tail, they churned through the snow as they ran across the pasture. Only one bull remained, feet planted wide, giving us a baleful stare. But it finally got to be too much for him too, and he ran to join the others.

Tucker stopped at the barbed wire fence. I rode up beside him. "There's a gate at the end, over there." I pointed down toward the flat part of the pasture. "These two ranches used to be one. We left the gate."

Tucker nodded, and we walked the horses through the snow. Axel and Tucker rode side by side, whispering, but I veered a little way off from them. The cattle had trampled much of the snow, and we were at the gate in just a few minutes.

I got off the horse, pulled the gate open, and the guys walked past me, taking Mary's reins and leading her through. On the other side, I closed the gate and took the reins.

"I'll walk back. It's just through there." I pointed to a gap in the trees where the backside of the house was visible. "I need a little alone time."

Axel shot Tucker a look, but Tucker only shrugged. "Walk fast." Then he turned and spurred Storm forward. Axel looked back at me before moving off, but at a slower pace. He kept looking back at me, concern on his face, but I just couldn't deal with people right now.

It felt good to walk, to stretch my legs. Unless I was on my deathbed, I'd never spent that much time in one place, not doing something, not working. The exercise didn't make up for that or get the memories of sex and death out of my head, but it helped stabilize my teetering mood. I took a deep breath of the cold air, watching the snowflakes drift through the pines.

I wondered what would happen, now that they'd taken care of the sniper. I wondered who he was, if he was local or someone the fracking groups had brought in to make good on their promise to my father, to threaten me to intimidate him into not signing the bill he'd sponsored. And there was something else that nagged at me. *What if that single bullet really hadn't killed the strange wolf's partner?*

Wait. The fracking bill. What day is it? "Holy shit." I stopped short, and Mary almost bumped into me. The vote on the bill would have been yesterday. *If it had passed, did that mean I was in more danger or less? If they defeated it, was I in the clear?* If I wasn't, would they send someone else after me anyway, to punish Dad?

I took Mary to the shed. Axel and Tucker had already put Storm and Jane up, giving them food and water. Fiona was still in the sheep barn, looking up at me with reproachful eyes as she nursed her twins. I leaned over the edge of her pen.

"It's an inhospitable world out there, Fiona. You'll get out soon enough."

She didn't seem impressed by me, or my words, and turned back to her lambs. I sighed and led Mary to the last empty stall. I got her saddle off, plunking it onto the floor. I fed and watered my horse, looked at the saddle, and for the first time, walked away instead of putting it up—too tired to even think about doing it.

If I really was still in danger, I was just too damn exhausted and overwhelmed to care. My wolf-shifter bodyguards had survived with only minor wounds. They could handle anything that happened.

"Come on, Alina. You need some food and rest."

Tucker took my arm, leading me out of the barn. Axel closed

the door, and we headed across the yard. I noticed his limp and glanced up at him.

"Still just a flesh wound? Do you need a doctor?"

He shook his head. "It's really not that bad. The wound just needs a good cleaning, and I'll be good as new."

"I'm glad," I mumbled. "Any sign that the second guy made it down the mountain?"

The two men frowned and looked at each other. Axel shook his head. "Not sure. He would have had to make it down the mountain wounded, in a snowstorm, without the aid of a horse. Difficult. But we'll keep watch, just in case."

"Thank you. I just can't anymore." I was emotionally and physically gutted.

❧   13   ❧

I looked up at my house, never so glad to be home. The tension in my body left, and I felt the muscles in my face easing, my mouth curving involuntarily into a smile. Elizabeth might not be here to cook, but I could manage a passable breakfast of eggs with all the fixings for the three of us. *Then, a long hot bath and bed.*

A flicker of heat passed through me, and I wondered if that bed might include Tucker and Axel. Then I shook my head. *What happened in the cabin is going to stay in the cabin.* All three of us had let our guards down, played out a brief fantasy, but now we were back in the actual world.

I looked up as the front door opened, and Henry stepped out, followed closely by a man in a baseball cap. Benny—Axel and Tucker's employee, the ex-sniper who had provided security in our absence.

Benny's face was pale and almost blank, eyes flicking from me to the back of Henry's head. His baseball cap appeared soaked, and there were water spots on his jacket, as if he'd just warmed up from being out in the snow.

I started to speak but stopped. Henry should have been glad to see me, and while that might have included nothing resembling a smile, I wasn't sure why he was glaring at me. It was almost like he was trying to scare me away with his gaze.

"Henry? Are you okay?" I stepped onto the bottom porch step, looking up at him. "Henry?"

The man in the cap pushed Henry forward, and that was when I saw the gun he had jammed into Henry's back. Axel tackled me, pushing me into the snow to protect me.

"Benny? What the hell?" Tucker demanded.

"Everyone stays calm, and he stays alive." Benny gestured to Henry, then looked down at me. "I want her. Give Alina up peacefully, and the old guy goes free."

"His name is Henry, and no, I'm not going with you." I struggled to my knees in the snow. Axel had already pulled a pistol from his jacket and moved in front of me, the gun trained on Benny. I'd lost track of Tucker, but then I saw movement on the other side of the porch. Benny saw it too, wrapped an arm around Henry's neck, and pulled back, the gun sandwiched between their bodies. If Tucker or Axel tried a shot, they'd shoot Henry in the process, and then Benny would finish the job. I got to my feet, and Axel moved again, putting himself between Benny and me.

I heard a dripping sound in the long silence that followed. *Blood.* It was coming from Benny, which was why his face was so white. He was bleeding from the silver bullet Axel had put in him up at the cabin.

He laughed and then coughed painfully, red flecks appearing on his whitened lips. "You guys should see your faces. You're so fucking naïve. Never thought I'd take a contract behind your back, did you?"

"You've got a silver slug in your lung, Benny. You won't survive if it's not removed. Give up, and we'll get you to the local bear-shifters. One of them's a medic." Axel was trying to be the voice of reason. "No amount of money is worth ending up dead."

Benny sneered. "So says the millionaire who wants for nothing, while the rest of us have to hustle for our next meal."

"You fucking traitor," I shouted.

He glared at me. "Shut up, cunt. You're not living past today, so you had better behave, or I'll make your death slower than it has to be."

Axel bared his teeth. "There are two of us and one of you, Benny. The odds aren't in your favor."

Benny snorted. "You have no shot. You shoot me, this guy's as good as dead."

Tucker was at the other end of the porch from us, about ten feet away from Benny. He had his gun out, finger on the trigger. He meant business, and I wondered just how good of a shot he was. My heart was beating a sickening tattoo against my ribs. Henry was my family, and he had a gun in his back because of me.

"Why the fuck would you betray us for money?" Axel was trying to keep Benny talking while Tucker sought a better angle.

Benny sneered. "I'm living paycheck to paycheck because of my gambling debts, while you and Tucker are living the good life."

"We gave you a job when no one else would." Axel took half a step forward, gun still trained on Benny and Henry.

"This isn't a job. You and Tucker said it's a probationary gig to see if I'm still up to snuff. I got my dignity. You two are acting like your shit don't stink. Acting like you're better than me. Well, I'm the best fucking sniper in the world."

Axel snorted. "You mean you used to be before you started hitting the bottle hard."

"Fuck you. I am the damn best sniper you've ever met. That's why those big oil boys offered me a ton of money, along with that idiot 'local guide' Shamus they hired for me to get rid of this human bitch." He grinned. "Imagine my surprise when you and Tucker hired me to babysit the property of my mark... Her. This gig should have been the easiest job ever, until you two idiots took the assignment to protect her yourselves, instead of sending someone else from your team."

The second man had been Shamus. He'd probably jumped at the chance to kill me as some sick revenge.

Axel took another step toward Benny. "I think we can talk about this…"

Benny's eyes turned wild. "Stay back." Benny backed up, pulling Henry with him.

Suddenly, everyone was moving, shouting. Axel ran forward with clothes shredding like confetti as he shifted into his wolf. Henry threw himself down onto the porch. Benny lunged after him. Tucker leaped for the gun. There was a struggle, and a whistling shot flew over my head. Benny was up, diving off the edge of the porch, heading straight for me.

Terrified, I froze.

Benny caught me around the waist, yanking me down to the ground. We rolled, and I ended up with my face shoved in the snow, ice crystals in my mouth and nose. I tried to breathe, but Benny's weight held me down, crushing my chest. He seemed to get heavier, denser, pushing me deeper into the powder. I was drowning in the snow.

Where his arm wrapped around my waist, I felt his hand changing from fingers to something thick. Claws raked through my jacket and shirt, grazing my skin, leaving fiery trails of pain. I tried to scream, but the snow was everywhere. There was nothing I could do but struggle weakly against him.

The weight was suddenly lifted. I pushed myself up on my hands and knees. Tucker as a wolf-shifter was rolling in the snow with a giant gray wolf. Coughing and wiping snow off my face, I screamed when something bumped into me. It was Henry, pulling me up out of the snow and half dragging, half carrying me to the edge of the porch.

"Are you okay?" Henry yelled. "Did that thing hurt you?"

"No. I'm okay," I answered with trembling fingers. Fear and adrenaline were still coursing through my veins. We leaned against each other, watching the fight unfolding in the yard. I felt as though I could not breathe, terrified of how this battle might end.

I watched in fear as Tucker's wolf lunged at Benny, ducking beneath his snapping jaws. Benny was a small wolf, but his moves were quick as he swung at Tucker, his massive fangs slicing the air.

I caught a flash of fur and fangs—Axel had shifted into his wolf form and went barreling toward Benny. There was a flurry of flying claws, growls, and snarls, and then Benny was on the ground, roaring with rage.

Axel went in hard, grabbing Benny by the neck, but the sniper twisted, using his superior speed to roll onto his feet. He shook his head, and Axel lost his grip, scrambling for a foothold in the crusty snow. His leg was bleeding again. But even more blood dripped from Benny's chest.

Tucker's wolf crouched and jumped, but Benny spun, and Tucker hit him with a glancing blow, barely stopping the wolf, but landing hard on the ground.

With a final snarl, Benny turned and bolted down the driveway toward the road. Axel and Tucker gave chase, but just as Benny reached the blacktop, a big pickup truck towing a trailer of hay bales lumbered around the corner, well above the speed limit. Benny dashed blindly across the road, the truck mere feet away. He must have been relying on his speed to get across, but his wound made him stumble at just the wrong moment.

Axel and Tucker came to an abrupt stop, and they could only watch the action unfold, ducking into the shadows before the driver saw them.

I caught the surprised expression on the driver's face as he slammed on the brakes to avoid hitting Benny, but it was too late. The truck smashed into the enormous wolf, and Benny flew through the air, landing in a crumpled, broken heap. When his body finished rolling, it lay motionless on the side of the road.

He was dead.

Henry and I collapsed to the ground, both of us panting for breath. I was a mess, tears running down my face, relief flooding my veins. We held on to each other.

"It's okay," Henry told me. "He can't hurt you anymore."

I was too overwhelmed to answer. In the back of my head, I wondered why Henry wasn't freaking out about the wolves, but I couldn't put the words together to ask.

We finally scrambled to our feet and walked down the driveway, Henry already recovered enough from his hostage situation to lend me his arm when I staggered.

The driver, clearly shaken up, pulled up to where we stood, rolled down his window, and leaned out. "Did you see that? Those damn coyotes are getting more and more aggressive. I swear in the last week, I've seen more tracks than I have my entire life." He squinted at me, then Henry. "I didn't mean to hit it, but I'm lucky the big bastard didn't roll my truck and take me with it. You two all right? It didn't attack you, did it?" His eyes widened in alarm, fear in his voice. We must look like hell. From the smell wafting off him, he was quite drunk, but what had just happened had sobered him a lot.

I shook my head, not bothering to correct him about the "coyote" he had killed. "We're okay. Just trying to get my horse back in the barn." I waved a hand in the vague direction of the sheep barn. "Must've gotten spooked by the...um, coyote."

The driver nodded, smiling his relief. "Well, good to see you, Alina. Sorry to hear about the barn. If you need anything, you just come on over and ask. I'll be back with the boys to collect the hide. Never seen a coyote with a coat that color."

I nodded, wondering who the hell the driver was—I'd never met him before—and forced a smile as he tipped his hat and pulled away. I watched him drive down the road, wondering if he'd be disappointed to find the corpse missing when he got back, then I turned to Henry.

"You okay?" I asked. "What the hell happened up here?"

Henry scowled. "That bastard showed up wounded after

going missing all night. Came down the mountain on the trail you used and left red dots all across the pasture. I saw he was bleeding and figured the sniper had gotten him. He got the drop on me when I went for the medical kit. Two-faced prick."

We started back up the drive. I wanted to look for Tucker and Axel, but I figured they knew best how to get themselves back to the house unseen. A sudden wave of laughter overtook me. Henry turned, a bemused look on his face.

"You all right, Miss Glory?"

"I just..." I was laughing hard now, a little hysterically. "You know, when they shift back into humans, they don't have any clothes on, so they're buck naked." I shook my head, tears running down my face. There was no way I could explain to Henry the image in my mind of two guys, stark naked, sneaking through the snowy fields back to the house.

"Yeah, these shifters have it rough." He spat into the snow. "Feel sorry for them sometimes."

I stopped and stared at Henry, mouth open in a most unlady-like fashion. "You know? About them—about shifters?"

"Well, there's a reason I didn't freak out when they shifted in front of me." He smiled and then winked at me. "And I know lots of things, Miss Glory. More than you'll ever know." The smile grew, and he walked away toward the house, leaving me dumbfounded.

❧ 14 ❧

Axel and Tucker were in the kitchen, already dressed, or at least Tucker was. Axel had my massive velvet throw blanket wrapped around his waist. For a minute, it confused me, until I remembered they'd left the rest of their clothes behind at the cabin. Axel bent over the kitchen sink, washing his face and chest with soap and water. He turned off the faucet, and I handed him a kitchen towel.

"Thanks. Glad to get rid of the scent of that bastard." He dried his face and chest, then nodded at Henry. "Nice work back there. You handled yourself pretty well."

"I didn't see everything. What happened?" I pulled out a chair and dropped into it. Henry grabbed a couple coffee cups, placed them on the table, and set down the big coffeepot. Axel and I reached for a cup, and I poured us each a steaming serving of black coffee.

"Henry executed a pretty competent martial arts move that got Benny's gun out of his back. Henry, start from the beginning. When did Benny tip his hand?" Axel shifted in his chair, wincing. I gave him a look of concern, but he shook his head. "When did you know?"

"He never really did," Henry replied. "I thought there was

something different about him not long after you left. Just a hunch, though. I let him think I was just an old man, doddering around." Henry shrugged. "I did what any good soldier would do. Waited for my chance and took it."

"Not bad, keeping your nerve like that, especially once the fangs came out." Axel looked at Henry curiously but then just smiled.

"It was the only thing I could do. Needed to look out for Miss Glory." He rubbed the side of his nose, and I knew it embarrassed him.

I stared at Henry through a mist of tears. He nodded at me, gave me a hint of a smile, and then ducked his head. I glanced down into my coffee, wondering how I'd gotten so lucky, and why I didn't know more about the man who'd twice risked his life for me.

Tucker pushed away from the counter. "I'm going to call the bear-shifters and let them know what happened." He turned to me. "Axel and I are not leaving until there's some resolution to this whole mess."

"You're stuck with us for the duration, I'm afraid." Axel pushed his coffee away and rose with visible effort.

I nodded. His words filled me with a mixture of emotions—joy, uncertainty, and nervousness—which all ran through me. Axel, Tucker, and I had unfinished business, and I wanted to at least clear the air between us.

I stood, striding toward Axel. "I need to look at that flesh wound."

Axel shook his head. "I've had worse. It'll heal."

"Upstairs with you, shifter." I jabbed a finger at him. "I need to see the wound for myself."

"Who am I to argue when a pretty girl asks me to take off my clothes?" He cocked an eyebrow as I sputtered indignantly. "Lead on. I'm all yours."

He followed me upstairs, and I steered him to my bedroom. "Sit." I pointed to my bed. "I'm getting something to clean your injury and bandage it." Turning on my heel, I headed to my master bathroom.

"Alina?"

I turned back to glare at him. "What?"

"Shouldn't I be taking off this throw?" He was already untucking it from around his waist. I willed myself to look at his face, but my eyes strayed to what he was doing.

"Ah...yes." I put my hand on the doorframe. "I'll be right back."

I left to the rumble of his laughter. *What the hell am I going to do now?*

I stood in my bathroom, bandages and towels forgotten. I'd had sex with him and with his best friend. Closing my eyes, I leaned my head against the mirror.

Damn. This is really awkward. I didn't know shit about intimacy or commitment, not that Axel and Tucker gave me any impression that's what they wanted from me. Just sex, I could handle, but whatever was going on between the three of us seemed different.

I bit my bottom lip as my heart raced with anxiousness. My life had been fine before those two showed up. Now, it was complicated, and it wasn't going back to normal anytime soon. Even with both Benny and Shamus out of the equation, it still left me with two men I liked and respected, who were now my lovers.

What had happened between the three of us still resonated through my soul. Nothing that intense had ever happened to me with any man, let alone a pair of them.

I plopped down on the edge of the bathtub and just stared into space. Now that I'd had a taste of what it was like to be with Axel and Tucker, I didn't want to turn back. I wanted more of them. Not just on a sexual level, but on a true, relationship level. *But what did they want from me? From us?*

Standing, I turned on the water at the sink, wetting a towel, then grabbing a box of gauze and tape from the medicine cabinet before striding back into my room.

"I thought you got lost." Axel was sitting on the bed, propped up against the headboard with the throw draped across his lap, covering his cock.

I gasped at the ragged gash across his ribs.

"Benny caught me with a claw. It's healing but not fast enough." He arched a brow. "You know, I could just shift into my wolf, and it will speed up the healing process."

"You could, but not before I clean it." I sat on the edge of the bed. "And that wound on your leg." It was deep, but the edges were clean. It needed stitches, but that was a little beyond my capabilities. "Knife?" I dabbed at the dried blood with the towel. The muscles in his leg twitched, and I knew the cut hurt.

"Yes. I surprised him, and the gun went off. The shot went wild. He swung the knife at me, and I was a little slow getting out of the way."

I nodded. "We heard that." I cleaned the wound and put antibiotic ointment on a gauze pad, pressed it on the gash, and then wrapped tape around it. "That's the best I can do for that. Even without shifting, you heal faster than humans, right?" I refolded the towel, leaning in to look at his chest. That cut was shallow with ragged edges. The blood was still fresh, and I cleaned away as much as I could. I stuck another wad of gauze on it and taped it in place.

"Yeah, the only reason the leg wound hasn't closed is that I was running around so much." He winced slightly.

"Guess I have nothing to worry about, then." I moved to stand, but he took my hand.

"Don't go. I think we need to talk." His dark eyes held mine, and I had no choice but to look at him.

"Yes. We do." My heart started a trip-hammer beat, and I took a breath, trying to quell the rising emotions inside me.

"Something special happened in that cabin, Alina. You know it. And so do I. We had something—"

"The three of us had something," Tucker's voice interjected.

I jerked my head toward the door. Tucker was leaning against the frame, arms crossed. He pushed away from the door, closing it, and crossed to the bed.

"But what do we do now?" I croaked.

"We do what we want, Alina. We're three consenting adults." Axel squeezed my hand. "I know what I want."

"So do I." Tucker sat beside me on the bed, resting his hand on my leg. "You're an incredible woman, Alina, even if you are hardheaded." He squeezed my leg as I scowled at him.

I knew what I wanted, but I wasn't ready to give myself over to them again without knowing more.

"This isn't a game with me, guys," I confessed. "I've never multitasked my way through a relationship before. I'm a one-man woman. This is all unfamiliar territory for me. And when you come down to it, I don't know either of you." Axel quirked an eyebrow, but I ignored him. "For all I know, you bed all your women clients."

"We don't, Alina," Tucker answered, reaching for my other hand. I let him take it. "I've had a lot of lovers, casual lovers, in the past. Shared some of them with Axel. But I don't want casual with you. I want this to be something more."

He pulled me to him, and I resisted, but only a little. I didn't want to open my heart again, only for it to get crushed by them.

I turned to Axel, catching the look of desire that flashed across his face, the passion shining in the dark depths of his eyes. "And you? Same story? Girl in every port? String of broken hearts?"

"I've had my share of conquests, same as Tucker, and yes, we've shared some of our lovers. But we don't sleep with clients. I don't mix business with pleasure." He tucked a strand of hair behind my ear. "Tucker is right. You're not what I expected, and you're worth taking a risk for."

I turned to Tucker. "So, you're breaking your own rules about not sleeping with clients...for me?"

Tucker laughed. "You could put it that way, I suppose."

Axel chuckled. "Besides, if you want to get technical, we volunteered for this. It was never really business at all. We took this job because we owed the bear-shifters a favor."

Tucker eyed Axel, and he nodded. "We also should tell you something..."

"What?" I asked.

"We don't want to freak you out..." Tucker started.

"Well, you are," I rebutted. *Were they married or something?*

"Alina, we're both in agreement that you're our true mate."

"True mate? What the hell is that?"

"It's the equivalent of a soul mate. Every shifter has a partner. Someone they're destined to love and protect—for the rest of their life. You are ours. It's rare for two shifters to have the same true mate, but here we are."

What. The. Fuck? "But how do you know that?" I squeaked.

"Your scent and the way you make our inner wolves feel. For the both of us, from the moment we've met you, our wolves have been yelling at us that you're ours."

I sat between them, between these two totally different men who wanted me and who believed I was their true mate. "This is a lot for me to process," I admitted.

"And that's why we waited to tell you this," Axel confessed. "You already had enough on your plate with your life in jeopardy. We didn't want to overwhelm you by revealing that you're our true mate."

Tucker trailed a finger across my cheek. "There's no pressure, Alina. If you want space, we'll give it to you. But we will not let you run away from this or us."

I arched a brow. "How does this work, with the three of us?"

Axel grinned. "We give you time to get to know us better. There's so much we want to tell you about our world. About us. And there's so much we'd love to learn about you."

"This will work, Alina," Tucker said, and Axel nodded. "And we will love, care for, and protect you until our dying breaths."

His words were beautiful, promising, and yet, overwhelming. I needed alone time to think. I stood up. "I need a shower. My house is your house. You can use the guest bathroom or the shower downstairs."

Tucker nodded. "Actually, that's not a bad idea. I'll take the downstairs." He left the room.

I turned to Axel. "Down the hall, last door on the left. There's shampoo and stuff in the shower, clean towels on the rack."

He eased himself off the bed. "I guess you'll just have to play nurse later and bandage me up again." I watched him limp down the hall. It wasn't something I'd mind, actually.

I headed toward my bathtub, running the water until it was almost scalding and pouring in a generous amount of lavender bath salts. Stripping off my clothes, I left them in an untidy pile on the floor as I turned off the water. My body felt bruised and beaten as I slid beneath the hot, scented water. I dipped my head briefly under the water to cleanse my hair then I popped back up into a sitting position.

While lathering my washcloth with a goat's milk bar soap scented with honey and orange blossom, I thought about what had happened, and might happen, with Axel and Tucker. I had the chance to explore something completely new. A relationship totally out of my comfort zone and considered taboo by society.

Am I willing to put myself out there with both of them?

Am I opening myself up to double the chance of a broken heart?

If I walk away, will I regret it?

Standing up, I stepped out of the tub, making sure the water was starting to drain before I dried myself off.

I knew that if I didn't give them a chance, I'd regret it. Besides, I didn't give a shit what people thought of our unorthodox relationship. I had one life to live, and I would let no one dictate how I would live it.

Smiling, I strode out of my bathroom, the towel wrapped around me, not altogether surprised to find both Axel and

Tucker in my bed, with a generous space between them, which I suspected was for me.

"We thought you'd decided to sleep in the bathroom." Axel grinned.

"Nope. I needed time to think." I noticed the bandage was back on his chest. I also noticed his hair was still damp, mussed up into dark waves. Tucker looked refreshed as well, if a little less damaged. He was lying on his side, the sheet pooled around his hips, giving me a long view of his flat stomach and that beautiful area below a man's navel, the deep V of the muscles of his hips, and then the sheet obscured the rest of the view. Seeing both of them, knowing they were both there for me, was a heady feeling.

I met Tucker's eyes and knew he saw right through me. Axel pulled back the sheet, an open invitation. I dropped the towel and walked toward the bed. I'd never been much of an exhibitionist, but watching them stare at me with adoration and lust in their eyes was powerfully intoxicating. But I wanted more than just their eyes on me.

Axel slid his legs over the edge of the bed, and I climbed in, careful not to jostle him. I glimpsed his thick erection and resisted the urge to wrap my fingers around it. It had been semi-dark in the cabin, all of us lit by just the glow of the fire. Here, in the full light in my room, I had an unfettered view of him. It excited me as I settled between them, pulling the sheet up as far as I could. I wanted to get out what I had to say without distractions.

"What did you think about?" Tucker stretched out beside me, letting the sheet slip carelessly down his body. It was pretty obvious he had the same thing on his mind that I did, that Axel did.

"I thought about the cabin. That what happened was way beyond anything I'd ever experienced."

"Was it good?" Axel reached out, hand on my thigh, fingers caressing me through the sheet. "I thought it was very good."

His voice was a deep growl, raspy, as though he strained to maintain control of himself.

"It was amazing. But it's not just the sex I was thinking about."

Axel tugged at the edge of the sheet. "What else were you thinking about?" The sheet slid down over my arms, and I grabbed at it, but Tucker twisted it again, and it slid lower, exposing one breast.

I swatted at him playfully. "Can I just say this without interruptions?"

"You can say anything you want, Alina. We're listening." Axel moved his fingers over my leg, taking up where Tucker had left off, pulling the sheet toward him, and away from me.

"What happened..." I pushed Tucker's hand away from my breast, just as Axel started caressing the other. "Cut it out. I'm talking here." He grinned, fingers stilling, but his hand remained resting on my breast.

I cleared my throat. "What happened was out of my comfort zone. I don't sleep with men without at least a first date."

Both men were quiet, their hands resting on my body. I had their attention, at least from the waist up.

"And I'd never had sex with two men...ever." I glanced between them. The dark and brooding Axel, and the rough and tumble Tucker. They couldn't have been more different, but they couldn't have been more exciting, more arousing, or handsome.

"I'm scared to death of getting my heart broken by you two." My voice sounded small, and I clutched the edge of the sheet. The guys stopped tugging at it, but they moved closer, arms reaching to hug me, to pull me close.

"What we have is real." Tucker's voice was low, and I slid down between them. Tucker brushed a strand of hair away from my forehead. "I've got just as much to lose as you do. My heart breaks just as easily as yours."

"I get that..."

He leaned down, kissing me softly, lips moving over mine.

After a minute, he leaned back. "Neither of us wants to hurt you. That's the last thing we want."

"Tucker's right. If this is what you want, then I want to give it everything I have. I want this to work." Axel turned my face to his, his kiss no less passionate than Tucker's, but firm and powerful.

Lust and passion and desire swirled around me, through me, and I kissed him back. I broke away, turning to Tucker, finding his mouth, kissing him greedily. I wanted them, both of them, all of them.

"Then we'll make it work," I said. "One more thing. Children." Under normal circumstances, it would be too soon to even broach this topic, but since we were going to take our relationship to the "serious and committed" level, it was better to talk about this now. "I want children. Not now, but eventually."

"I do too," Axel said.

"Ditto," Tucker chimed in. "Given your relationship with your dad, we didn't know what your stance on children was."

"He's a horrible father. My mother walked away—not only from him, but me—without looking back. So, granted, I don't have excellent role models for parents. But I want kids. I can give them the love, happiness, and caring that I never got but deserved." I paused. "I'm not ready for kids, but I will be someday."

They both grinned, eyes glowing with happiness. Without another word, the sheet fell away, and I was lying naked under the gazes of Axel and Tucker. I returned the favor, taking my time soaking in every inch of them, lingering over the curve of a bicep on one, the taut stomach muscles of the other, the arch and length of both erections. It was intoxicating, and I was drunk with choices.

Tucker reached for me, sparing me the decision of whom to kiss first. He held my face in his hands, lips on mine, tongue dancing in my mouth. I arched up, wrapping my hands around his neck, holding him to me.

It was different this time, the kiss. There was no howling blizzard or sniper waiting in the forest. We had nothing but time. I let myself sink into this moment, into the feel of his lips on mine. Hands began touching me in too many places to count. Tucker's arms ran down my back, hands cupping my ass. Axel reached around to cradle my breasts, one hand slipping lower.

Axel put just enough pressure on my hip to tip me onto my back. Tucker moved with me, rising over me, covering my breasts with his chest, and pressing me into the mattress. He bracketed my face with his hands, deepening the kiss.

Hands on my face, Tucker. *Check.*

Hands on my breasts, gliding lower, Axel. *Check.*

Axel skimmed his fingers over my thighs and not-so-gently pulled my legs apart. I gave him no resistance, arching my back and sliding my feet along the sheets, knees falling to the sides.

Axel kissed the inside of my knee, his tongue tracing circles over my skin. He worked his way higher, moving between my legs, side to side, giving equal attention to each thigh. I exhaled a sigh of contentment against Tucker's mouth, my head falling back. I ran my tongue over my lips, tasting Tucker.

"Too much for you? Rather have us one at a time?" Tucker asked.

"Hell no!" I responded.

There was a muffled chuckle against my leg, and Axel pushed himself up, looking at me from his spot farther down the bed. He cocked one eyebrow, resting his head on his hands.

"Are you sure?" Axel asked. "I'll wait...not patiently, but I'll wait."

I turned my head, looking up at Tucker. I gave him a lazy smile. "You guys aren't too much. You're just enough."

Tucker's mouth curved into a bad-boy smile. "Good answer." He moved beside me until his body rested against mine, his erection pressed into my hip.

Axel winked at me and then disappeared with a wicked grin. I felt his lips on my thigh, his tongue flicking farther north, teasing me. His hands slid beneath my ass, lifting me, opening me farther. I took a deep breath, letting it out slowly as his tongue glided over me, tasting me, licking and sucking, feasting on me until I lay gasping.

Tucker turned from watching Axel and lowered his head again, lips moving against mine, the kiss exquisite and slow, powerful and deep. I sank against the pillow, hands in his hair, kissing him, letting him kiss me, trying to kiss him back, interrupted by gasps of pleasure as Axel worked his magic between my legs.

I ran my hand down Tucker's chest, over all that warm skin and hard muscle, down over his stomach, then lower, brushing through the thatch of hair, to his massive erection. When I wrapped my hand around the thick shaft of his cock, his hips flexed forward, and I felt more than heard his deep moan against my lips.

I stroked him, letting his cock slide through my hand, trying to set a rhythm. But Axel had set a different rhythm between my legs, and I got distracted, wonderfully and amazingly distracted, from what I was doing to Tucker. My hand slowed, then stopped, still wrapped around him.

Tucker broke away from our kiss, his lips against my ear. "Let it go, Alina. Let it happen."

Axel was setting off a series of delicious shocks of lust between my legs, echoes running through my body, climbing higher, filling me with delicious heat. I was close to the edge. I knew it. Axel knew it, and Tucker did too.

Axel rose, moving quickly over my body, sliding his cock into me. I arched up suddenly, one hand tangled in the sheets, bucking against Axel as he thrust his cock into me. Tucker pressed against my side, kissing my forehead, nuzzling my neck, his breath hot against my skin.

"Yes..." I moaned. "More."

The first thrust was perfect, slow and hard, filling me completely. Axel pulled back gradually. I looked up at him, willing him to ravish me completely. He thrust faster, and I rose to meet him, wrapping my legs around his waist.

"Harder..." I begged.

Tucker teased kisses along my hairline, hand caressing my breast. I turned, kissing him, lips and tongue meeting. But it only lasted a moment before I broke away, looking up at Axel as he drove into me, over and over. The arousal in my body rose with each stroke, carrying me to the edge.

"Yes." I reached up, caressing his cheek. "I want this... I want all three of us forever. Make me yours."

Axel bent his head, lips crashing against mine, taking my breath away as he plundered my mouth. I threw my head back and groaned, my stomach tightening with pleasure as my climax approached.

Axel moaned against my mouth, broke away, and buried his face in the space between my neck and shoulder. His teeth sank into my skin, biting me before licking the sting away.

Tucker was close, his hands, fingers, and his tongue touching any place Axel was not. It was heaven. Beyond anything I could have ever imagined. Then Tucker nipped my neck before sinking his teeth between my neck and shoulder. I moaned in pleasure.

Axel lifted his head and grunted, "Mine."

I ran my hands down his back, feeling the muscles at his hips tense and flex as he came. He thrust hard and fast and then stayed buried inside me until his seed shot into me.

We were one big mess of arms and legs, hands and mouths, and I was the center of it all. Axel rolled off me, breathing hard. I sat up, pushing Tucker onto his back. My body was alive for round two.

I leaned over his hips, reaching greedily for his erection with both hands. I licked his cock like he was a feast and I was starving. He tasted salty and rich, and I lapped him up. I pulled him into my mouth while eyeing him. I loved the look on his face. His lips parted, breath rasping, our eyes locked. His expression mirrored the wantonness I felt inside.

Tucker rose on his elbow, reaching down, one hand behind my neck, fingers winding in my hair. There was pressure, gentle at first, his fingers caressing me as I swirled my tongue around the tip of his staff.

The pressure against my neck grew, forcing me down onto him imperceptibly. I was more than willing to go, to take him deep into my mouth. I swallowed, barely, and he filled my mouth. I snuck a hand between his legs, caressing his balls. Tucker jerked his hips upward with a harsh sound, his hand tightening against my head. I held his gaze, took a breath, and let him pull me down. My lips brushed against his body, him on the edge, me with the power to push him over the precipice of lust.

"Tucker, you taste so good."

I savored the moment, let it play out, held his gaze. He looked at me, and I waited, more patient than I ever thought I could be, doing everything I could with mouth and tongue, fingers and hands, until I saw him break. He was begging me with his eyes to let him come. I was heady with lust, power, excitement. These beautiful, powerful men worshiped and respected me as their equal, as their goddess.

He let go of my head briefly, and I pulled back as he thrust up. "Mine!" he growled before he came in my mouth. It was intense, explosive. Tucker roared as he filled my mouth. I couldn't swallow, didn't even try, watching him watch me, letting him see his offering run out of my mouth and down his hard shaft.

It all ended slowly, but far too quickly. I sat back, smiling, and wiped my mouth with the back of my hand. Tucker looked at me for a moment, then said, "Damn, you're beautiful and ours."

"And don't you forget it," I sassed back before bursting out laughing. Axel chuckled. I grinned at them.

"I told you I could handle both of you." I flopped down

between them, stretching my arms overhead. "So, this is how it's going to be, from now on?"

Axel turned on his side, head propped on his hand. "Yep, but are you sure this what you want?"

Tucker mirrored Axel's pose. Pure, intoxicating sexuality and overwhelming masculinity surrounded me.

I turned my head, looking between my two incredible lovers.

"Yes," I answered. "You two are mine..."

Christmas morning dawned to swirling snow outside and a big, warm body spooning me from behind. I stirred and lifted my head, looking out my repaired bedroom window at the white flakes drifting by. Outside, I could hear the joyful barks of my dogs playing. I'd slept in, but not by much. If the dogs were out, then Henry was already hard at work.

I marveled at how much my life had changed in such a short period. I'd learned many things about Axel and Tucker, including that they were the alphas of their pack of almost a dozen wolf-shifters.

Henry still wouldn't tell me how long he had known about the existence of shifters, but he'd stuck around when the bear-shifter cops had come by to wrap things up and take off with Benny's body. They informed me they were investigating the local wolf-shifter pack, just in case Shamus had an accomplice. They were guessing Shamus himself was behind threatening our local newspaperman, but until they knew for sure, their jobs were not done.

After the cops had left, my phone call to Dad had been short and curt. I recapped that the sniper and his arsonist accomplice had died trying to escape. The local cops were investigating. There was no sign of any more accomplices. Dad had told me that the anti-fracking bill was now law, and I'd congratulated him with my best professional voice, still feeling cold that his political career had advanced further at such a cost to me and mine. But then again, without the threat against me, I never would have met the loves of my life.

I also had gently but firmly rebuffed his latest "request"—more like a demand—that I come join him and his trophy wife in DC for Christmas. When he had mentioned a "promising lobbyist"—in his fifties—he wanted to introduce me to, I had informed him that I was not single or available. After that, I'd refused to answer any of his shocked questions, saying that I chose my own partners and that he should know better than to marry me off to someone nearly as old as he was.

Breaking out of my thoughts of the past, reluctantly, I got up, only to have the figure behind me grumble and sling a powerful arm around me, pulling me back against him.

"Too early," Tucker grumped sleepily in my ear. "You stay here now." He kissed the back of my neck, and I shivered, my resolve wearing away fast.

"We've got Elizabeth, her sons, Henry and his family, and an entire pack of wolf-shifters coming here and expecting dinner. Henry and Elizabeth can't do it on their own." I halfheartedly struggled against his grip until he sighed, letting me go. Axel and Tucker's pack members were eager to meet me, the woman who had captured the hearts of their alphas.

"Fine," he muttered, sitting up. "Now that the coffee's ready anyway."

I sniffed. I couldn't smell the coffee upstairs and through the door, but of course, Tucker could. "I'll take your word for it. You want the shower first?"

"No. You need a bigger shower so we can get in together."

A bigger shower to go with my new, bigger bed. The California king took up most of my snug bedroom, but at least it could fit all three of us comfortably. Axel and Tucker had surprised me two days ago with the bed and mattress delivery, and they had spent two hours putting the new frame together and loading the big thing onto it. After, we'd spent the evening christening it, until I was so exhausted that they had to tuck me in.

After showering and dressing, Tucker and I went downstairs. They had transformed the living and dining room, the smell of pine, cranberries, apple pie, and coffee filling the air. A fully trimmed tree with the angel topper brushing the ceiling sat in the corner, presents piled beneath it. Elizabeth had supplemented her Christmas lights with strings of glowing icicles and snowflakes. I hung the wreath on the back of the door with bells.

"Merry Christmas, sweetheart!" Elizabeth glided out of the kitchen in her long skirt and reindeer apron to give me a hug and a kiss on the cheek. "Axel has started the turkey. He's quite handy." She turned back briefly and brought us both our coffee, smiling. "Are you happy?" Elizabeth and Henry had adapted to and accepted the fact that I had two lovers, with no questions asked.

"Yes. Very happy." I grinned before taking a test sip of my coffee for temperature before downing most of the mug's contents.

"Good," she replied, "That's all I give a shit about, your happiness."

"That makes three of us—you, me, and Axel—Elizabeth." Tucker wrapped an arm around my waist while sipping his coffee.

I grinned. "Any news?" I asked Elizabeth.

"The builders will come by after New Year's to set up the modular barn. Meanwhile, Henry is letting the horses out to run as much as the weather allows. I don't think the sheep like their new roommates much, but we got three more lambs while you slept." She scratched her cheek, dislodging a fleck of piecrust dough.

I nodded. The modular would not be pretty, but until we rebuilt the horse barn, it would do better than cramming Storm and his girls in with the expanding sheep population. "I guess they can manage for another week. Where's Henry?"

"He and Axel are finishing morning chores so he can go open presents with his kids." At my guilty look, she held up a hand. "Now, don't do that. You needed proper rest after everything."

"I tried telling her that," Tucker grumbled between sips of coffee. "You know how hyperresponsible she is."

"Always." Elizabeth nodded. "Everything's ready or getting ready," she directed to me. "So, you'll just have to settle for enjoying your Christmas."

I huffed as Tucker gave me a smirk. "Well," I sighed. "Guess that's that, then."

"Told you," he chuckled before kissing my cheek.

I shoved him playfully. "You go make yourself useful."

"I thought I did...upstairs in bed." He gave me a naughty grin.

I swatted him, eyeing Elizabeth, who fanned me and walked away, laughing.

"Let's go, shifter," I ordered.

Both of us bundled up and headed outside into the snow. The horses, happy to be back home, were chasing one another through the ankle-deep fluff, while the dogs scrambled after a ball that Axel was throwing for them.

Despite the blackened bones of my barn looming over the scene, I felt a sense of peace washing over me. Tucker and Axel had done what they did and more. They had changed my life.

"Are you sure you want to stay at the ranch with me?" I asked softly as Tucker came to stand beside me.

"Well, it's a lot easier to move between here and our range

outside Billings when we have Axel's helicopter to ferry us back and forth." He gave me a sly smile. "Have you thought about what you'll be telling your father about us?"

"Nothing," I sighed. "It's none of his damn business."

"One of these days, you're going to have to tell him something," he warned me gently, and I shrugged.

"All my life, he's tried to use me as a means to an end, just like he did with my mother. His politics may have pissed off the crazy-neoconservative crowd, but he's as corrupt as they are. He just saves his amorality for his family." Which was why he didn't have a family anymore, just a wife-for-hire he'd cut loose with a nice chunk of alimony as soon as she hit forty, before moving on to the next one. "This mess with Benny, Shamus, and the guys who hired them is just the latest problem he's caused in my life. And all he could think of was to leverage it to get me back under control." I huffed out with exasperation. "No, the last thing I want to do is let him or anyone else in Washington know I'm in love with two men. He'd just try to meddle in our business, and we don't want that shit."

"You have a point, but Axel and I are not worried about him. We've got a legal team with very sharp teeth. One phone call from them, and he'll behave if he knows what's good for him." He winked, all confidence and amusement, and I felt a little better at once.

"I trust you two." Happy to have two hard-core "take no shit" men in my corner.

Axel came over to kiss me good morning, with the dogs milling around his legs. "Merry Christmas," he purred before nipping my bottom lip.

Raising up on my toes, I ran my fingers through his hair. "And a merry Christmas to you."

Wrapping his arms around my waist, he kissed me thoroughly. "You don't know how bad I want to carry you upstairs and have my freaky, dirty way with you."

My cunt pulsed with anticipation. "None of that," I whispered. "We have company coming."

He growled playfully before releasing me. "The pack should be here in a few hours. They insisted on driving down."

"Well, that's probably better than landing a helicopter in this weather." The near field was big and bare enough, but the snow cut visibility to a ridiculous degree. "Do they have a place to stay in town?" I had room to feed a dozen people but not room to bunk them.

"Yeah. I doubt the local pack will like it too much," Axel chuckled. "But they've got the bear-shifters on their back thanks to Shamus, so they may not even notice."

I frowned, hating any possibility of friction between Axel and Tucker's pack and the local pack.

"No frowning," Tucker ordered me. "Or worrying. Everything will be okay. Besides, it's Christmas."

I nodded, feeling comforted when they crowded around me protectively.

* * *

It was late in the afternoon when the pack started descending on us. Most were unrelated to one another, from what I could tell. Almost all were big, beefy guys with military backgrounds, and every one of them was friendly. None of them seemed shocked when Axel and Tucker told them I was their true mate.

Everyone gathered inside, sipping coffee or eggnog while the turkey finished roasting. I listened to them exchange war stories with one another and Henry, while I sat between my men and occasionally got up to play hostess. But Axel and Tucker refused to let me work too hard. Elizabeth wasn't working too hard because the pack members helped in the kitchen. Men rolling up their sleeves and helping by cooking, setting up the table, or filling everyone's glasses or mugs was a wonderful sight. But a strange feeling haunted me the entire time. It was only when we finally sat down to dinner and Tucker started carving up the bird that I could identify what the feeling was. It was the total absence of loneliness and depression. This was the first Christmas since Mom had left that I wasn't moping my way through the day and struggling to hide it.

Tucker set an enormous slab of breast meat and a pile of stuffing onto my plate. "Eat up, darling. You'll need your strength for later," he said bluntly. I blushed, and a ripple of laughter rang around the adult table. At the children's table filled with Henry's and Elizabeth's kids, they were eating and gabbing.

I glanced at Axel and saw the heat in his eyes as he stared back at me. I was definitely getting another Christmas gift later...and it was going to be a big one.

"So," Tucker started once I had tucked into my food. "What do you think of Christmas now?"

I smiled after chewing and swallowing my mouthful of turkey. "This is a vast improvement on the Washington parties, I have to admit."

It was more than that. Far more. Dad's absence in past years hadn't been enough to lift my depression, though it had been better to be lonely out in Montana than at a crowded DC party. But for the first time, I was actually happy on Christmas.

"Well, that's definitely a start. Anything we can do to improve on the situation?" Axel was fighting a grin.

"Not much, besides passing the cranberry sauce." I winked at him.

My life had gotten a lot more interesting in the last two weeks, and it promised to become more so now that Tucker and Axel were part of it for good. I knew that, from now on, "interesting" would be something to look forward to. Tucker and Axel would fill my life with love, happiness, joy, and shifters, and I could think of nothing better.

* * *

Thank you for reading **SHIFTERS FOR THE HOLIDAY**! **Read HOLIDAY FUREVER** for more warm and **fuzzy goodness!**

GET A FREE SEDONA VENEZ BOOK!

https://sedonavenez.com/free-book

ABOUT THE AUTHOR

USA TODAY BESTSELLING AUTHOR SEDONA VENEZ lives in New York City with her hot ex-military hubby—hooah—and their fur babies. She loves writing sizzling, sexy intricate stories about strong but broken characters who push limits, overcome their fears and risk it all for love.

Sedona loves to connect with readers!
www.sedonavenez.com